THE ART OF
RAISING HELL

THE ART OF RAISING HELL

Thomas Lopinski

Dark Alley Press

The Art of Raising Hell

© 2015 by Thomas Lopinski

ISBN: 978-0-692-37573-0

Dark Alley Press
http://www.darkalleypress.com

An imprint of Vagabondage Press LLC
PO Box 3563
Apollo Beach, Florida 33572
http://www.vagabondagepress.com

First edition printed in the United States of America and the United Kingdom, May 2015

10 9 8 7 6 5 4 3 2 1

Front cover art by Adam Hicks and Groupera. Cover designed by Maggie Ward.

THE ART OF
RAISING HELL

This book is dedicated to the memory of Joe Dill, and to the four guys who made the Backroom come alive.

Special thanks to:

Cathy Dill and her entire family, Warren Cravens, Doug Weaver, John Lopinski, Mark Brittingham, Greg Pribble, Becky Pribble, Laurel Carpenter, Barbara Carter, Debbie Potter, Michael Scherenberg, Jim Gleichman, Gary Emmert, Stacy Grover, The Guys and Gals of Raise Hell Blaisdell, Sully, Anna Lopinski, Lisa Lopinski, N. Apythia Morges, my family, all of the people at Vagabondage Press, and a very special thank you to John "Chris" Gleichman who's been there from the beginning to be my guiding light, my cheerleader, my devil's advocate, my creative spark, and, most of all, my dearest friend.

THE ART OF
RAISING HELL

Chapter One

"There are some people that walk around on two feet and others like me that run on all four."

To most people, that's a bold statement. I just wish I'd been the one to say it, but I wasn't. In fact, until a few days ago, I wasn't even sure what it meant. And if that's not strange enough, I'll let you in on another little secret: It's probably not what you think.

You might say that, on the surface, it's a very simple concept: Either you're the type of person who lives within a set of boundaries or the type who knows none. But life is never that simple, is it? No, I'd say that the most important insights about who we are, what we say, and why we do things are not always the obvious ones. Instead, they're discovered on the streets of your hometown, revealed late at night in a dark backroom, or sometimes forced upon you at knifepoint where your only choices for survival are between bad and worse.

The one person that knew no boundaries in Bunsen Creek was Lonny Nack. At the time when he proudly delivered that line, I didn't give it much thought. You see, he was the type of guy who loved to hear himself talk. Half the time, his words seemed larger than life. Other times, he just rambled on until he ran out of breath. It didn't matter, though. He was always entertaining.

I mean, the man had a saying for everything:

"That's slicker than snot on a glass door knob."

"I could sell a drowning man a glass of water."

"The more you keep stirring an old turd, the more it stinks."

"Just because you have a crack up your ass doesn't make you a cripple."

The list goes on.

Yet, that one phrase, that daring metaphor about people who don't walk around on two feet, did grab my attention. So much that I wanted to know, with all my heart, if he was really chasing some elusive level of enlightened bliss or running away from it.

I know now.

And I hope by telling you his story, you'll understand how it was that his life became entangled with mine, forever.

Allow me to explain.

This story begins five years ago when I was a newly minted teenager in the second year of a new decade. It was the 1970s in the Midwest, and I was ready to take on the world. I wasn't your typical wallflower who kept his head down in the hallway or cradled *The Catcher in the Rye* under his pillow at night. No, it's safe to say that I was quite the opposite. When I hit puberty, a whole new world order of romance and mischief opened up for me that most kids could only dream about.

But there was the other side of growing up that I wasn't even close to figuring out: the hormonal urges, the awkward conversations, and that "special" girl who made me believe, made me wonder, and made me feel. Then there were the different paths we cross in life, never quite knowing which one to take, which friends to make, and which enemies to avoid. Add to that the loss of the one person who meant the most to me, and you had one screwed up teenager.

I still remember what my mother said—God rest her soul—that morning when I turned thirteen and asked what was so different about today as opposed to yesterday.

"Well," she said in a perky tone while rubbing her belly, "becoming a teenager is kind of like giving birth. After months of preparation and pain, all of a sudden, you've created a new human being. But, instead of it being a helpless, little baby, you've created a full-grown person."

My shoulders gently collapsed as I exclaimed, "What the heck kind of advice is that? That's about as useful as dried up spit."

She took my hand, brushed back my bangs, and said something that I'll never forget: "My sweet son, no matter how much you learn from books and teachers, in the end you must give birth to that voice deep down inside of you. It will tell you what is right and what is wrong. Just follow that inner voice."

"You mean my soul?"

She smiled and gently nodded. "They are one and the same."

"So…when I give birth to this inner voice, am I going to have labor pains and grow big breasts or start eating pickles or cry for no reason in the middle of a movie theater?"

She chuckled. "Don't ever lose that sense of humor. It'll come in handy when you get older."

For the last five years, I've been trying to find that inner voice. Unfortunately, I've come up with nothing, nada, diddly-squat, zilch…until now. I don't know why it took so long. Maybe it was because, after she died, I did everything in my power to deny it for the longest time. Maybe I just wasn't ready. Or maybe, it took meeting Lonny, that one person, that kindred spirit and friend, who could make that "voice" be heard.

It's his words, along with my mother's, that guide me now. To say that he changed my life is an understatement. Hell, he made me into a local hero twice and almost got me killed! Fate being what it is, I sit here now telling you this story as I, literally, ride off into the sunset. But if it hadn't been for Lonny and those few simple words, that might not have been the case.

Chapter Two

The first time I met Lonny Nack was when I was in junior high, just a few months after moving to town. Baseball practice had just wrapped up, and I was unchaining my bicycle from the rack. As I placed my backpack on the handlebars, I heard a horse whinnying behind me. Naturally, I spun around, waiting for the oncoming stampede, when, to my surprise, a tanned, shirtless young man, maybe fifteen or sixteen, sporting a mohawk haircut sat on a giant horse, holding the reins. He had the sculptured high cheekbones of a Cherokee, but the rest of his face could have easily been lifted off a Paul Newman head shot, right down to the blue eyes. He leaned back on the horse as it danced on the pavement, oozing charisma like it was lava flowing down from a mountainside.

"Didn't mean to scare you, kiddo."

I was at a complete loss for words. The sight was so mindboggling that it took me a while to comprehend what I was looking at. I mean, who in their right mind brought a horse into town these days? It wasn't until I noticed the snake wrapped around his belly that I fully understood why I was speechless. It must have been at least ten feet long, light brown with dark spots every few inches, with a circumference the size of a grown man's bicep.

"It's a python," he boasted. "I call her Betsy. Not even sure if it's a girl or a boy, but the name seemed to fit." The snake's head slithered across the horse's mane as I took two steps backward. "Don't worry; she won't bite. Just don't let her get too comfortable around your neck, if you know what I mean."

Just then, the snake swung around his shoulder and landed on his back instantly securing a chokehold around his neck. Lonny's face quickly turned a shade of red only seen on a call girl's lips. Gurgling sounds flowed out of his mouth, while foam dripped from the sides. The more he tried to pull away from the snake, the redder his face turned.

I didn't know what to do. As this horrible spectacle unfolded before my eyes, I stood there, still dumbstruck. Lonny was now leaning back on the saddle as the snake's head swung around full circle, looping into the final kill position. With Lonny's head staring up at the cobalt sky, spit shot into the air as he gasped for breath. Finally, my instincts lunged me forward, and I reached out to grab the snake's tail, but the horse wildly swung around, blocking my advance. Now, I was on the other side of the saddle. Then it happened. There we were, face to face. The snake staring me down with its cold, black, lifeless eyes, surely wondering how tasty a dessert I'd make after making a meal out of Lonny.

This is it, I thought. *I'm gonna die. Thirteen years down the drain, and I haven't even gotten to third base with a girl yet.* What a tragic ending to such a promising life. I could already see the headlines in tomorrow's newspaper: "Two Youths Strangled by Python. Killer Still at Large."

Then I heard someone call, "Lonny, stop teasing him."

I recognized that voice. It was Sally Nack. One of the cutest girls in my class with the nastiest right hook you'd ever seen. She'd proven her toughness many times on the playground when boys tried to boss her around. Maybe she was a bit rough around the edges, but man, was she ever blessed with the prettiest set of green eyes and the most gorgeous long, thick, blonde hair. Every boy my age wanted to go steady with her but was too afraid to ask. That, of course, just made her even meaner as she was coming into womanhood and ready to hang up those boxing gloves for a set of curlers and a date at the movies.

"Dammit, Sally, it was just starting to get good. I really had him fooled."

That's when I realized they were talking about me. I was the patsy here. He'd reeled me in, hook, line, and sinker, like a starving, blind carp in a bathtub.

Sally put her hand on my shoulder. "Sorry. That's my idiot brother there. He loves to get people's blood boiling."

Lonny let out a laugh, half humorous, half apologetic. "Ah, no blood, no foul. Right, kid?"

Still looking for the first words to come out of my mouth, I gathered up whatever shards of dignity I had left and replied, "No blood, no foul."

"There you go, Sis. I kind of like this kid. What's your name?"

"Ryan. Ryan Johnson."

"You must be Hector's boy. My dad does business with your dad."

That was Lonny's polite way of saying that my father liked to buy things secondhand. With the new house and all, finances were tight, so any time my dad found a bargain, he went for it. The Nack family lived in the last house on the edge of town, next to the railroad tracks. It was one of those big two-story wooden homes ordered straight out of a Sears & Roebuck catalog during the 1920s. The long front porch was the first thing that caught your eye, with its intricate wooden railing, sleek vertical columns and squeaky but comfortable swing. The corners were accented with lilac bushes while vibrant arrays of flowerpots welcomed you up the front steps. There was a parlor, dining room, living room, kitchen, four bedrooms upstairs, and servant's quarters downstairs. Of course, the servants moved out sometime during the Depression and never came back. Still, with all of its hardwood beauty and charm, it was no match for the daily 4 o'clock train from Chicago that came barreling through town, rattling loose every nail and two-by-four within those walls.

Joseph Nicolas Nack owned and ran a junkyard of sorts called "Nick's Nacks." The name was so fitting that you could only imagine he'd been destined to be a junk collector from birth. It also helped weed out the traveling salesmen and shysters who came a-calling. Anyone who knew Joseph knew better than to call him "Nick." The minute someone walked through the door yelling, "Hello, Nick," Joseph knew what he was dealing with.

The man had almost every kind of item in the world buried somewhere in that huge barn out back of his place. You name it, from army medals to arm chairs, pinball machines to washing machines.

All of them could be found there, and if he didn't have it in stock, he'd find it for the right price. He'd cornered the market on second-hand stuff, that's for sure. What made his place so different was that he only carried quality items, and once they were cleaned up and polished, they were almost as good as new. The only competition within miles was Dukas's Clothing Store on the square. It wasn't really a competition as far as most folks were concerned though. If you wanted new socks, you went to Dukas's. If you wanted a used dresser to put them in, you went to Nick's.

After my father took a new job selling insurance for Metropolitan Life, he moved us from our tiny apartment into a nice-sized house in Bunsen Creek. My dad and Joseph met at his shop and hit it off immediately. Even though they were a generation apart in age, they were both widowers, alone and pissed off at the world, God and all, for stealing the loves of their lives. I didn't know that Sally even had an older brother. The fact that Lonny had been away at a youth detention facility for the last two years wasn't the kind of small talk brought up casually. Sally would later fill me in on the backstory of how he was given the choice of a youth detention center or a thousand dollar fine. Well, it wasn't really Lonny's choice. There was no way Joseph was going to cough up a thousand dollars just to save his boy's sorry ass. No, nothing else had worked up to then, so Joseph thought maybe a little "quality time" away from home would teach him a lesson.

But it didn't.

"Well, glad to meet ya." Lonny leaned down, reached out his lion's paw, and shook my hand. "Sorry about old Betsy here. Someone brought this rubber snake into the shop a few weeks ago, and I just had to have a little fun with it. See, it swings in three different sections." Then he pointed out one of the indentations where a hinge was concealed.

"You sure had me fooled, you know, foaming at the mouth and all."

"Club soda." He reached around to a side flap on the saddle overflowing with metal pots and pans, pulled out a bottle, opened it, and took a swig. "Ahhh, works every time." Then he looked to his sister and said, "You ready?"

"Yep. You been dumpster diving again?"

Lonny tried to stuff the utensils back down into the saddlebags. "One man's trash is another man's treasure."

Sally latched onto Lonny's arm as he swung her up and seamlessly placed her on the back of the saddle. Then he wrapped the rubber snake around his waist, yanked on the reins, and winked.

"Catch you later."

Sally didn't say a word as they rode off. She just flipped her hair behind her ears, flashed me a sheepish grin, and turned away. It might have been just a smile to her, but to me, it was Juliet on the balcony in a soft light through yonder window, it was a gondola ride through the canals of Venice, and, most importantly, it was all the reason I needed to fall in love.

That summer was special in many ways. Not only did I meet the soon-to-be infamous Lonny Nack, I also met the three best friends a person could have asked for. I don't know exactly why they took me into their little gang. I knew it wasn't my charismatic personality, because I didn't have one. It wasn't about money, because I didn't have any of that either. Maybe it had something to do with the annoying problem of always having a third wheel in the group instead of a foursome. After all, with just three people, there was always an odd man out. Yeah, I bet it was more out of necessity than anything else. Either way, it was the best thing that ever happened to me.

Before they allowed me to hang out though, they had to give me a nickname. I was told that it was part of a tradition handed down from Skeeter's older brother who'd bequeathed the Backroom, our designated hangout, to him before he'd left for college. Later on, I realized that Skeeter and T.J. had always had nicknames from the time they were born, so they probably gave Buzzard one just so he didn't feel left out.

"Okay, what are we going to call you?" asked Skeeter. "No significant scars, birthmarks, or tattoos."

"Let's call him 'Noscar' or 'Tattless'," jested Buzzard.

"Noscar! Sounds like something Poncho Villa would name his dog."

Feeling a bit uncomfortable, I asked, "How'd you come up with Buzzard's name?"

"That's easy," replied T.J. "He stares like a freaking Buzzard, and those glasses make his pupils look huge."

Skeeter jumped up, patted me on the back, and said, "I got it. He's new in town and the newest kid in school. Let's call him Newbie." The name stuck like a tick on a hound dog.

The next few years were the best time of my life. A foursome was the perfect combination for wicked games of whiffle-ball and basketball. Plus, when we went into Buck's Diner for lunch or soda pops, we didn't have to worry about some other goofball from class trying to squeeze into a seat at our table. We shared everything, from sandwiches to girlfriends. Learning as we went along, thinking we knew it all, and coming up with just enough bullshit to convince everyone else that we were in complete control of the situation. Of course, nothing was further from the truth, except for maybe Skeeter.

Skeeter had a demeanor about him that just screamed calm, cool, and collected. He was your class clown, international playboy, and occasional juvenile delinquent all rolled into one. I couldn't even begin to tell you how many times that quick wit and charm had gotten us out of a jam and saved our butts. Unfortunately, the rebel in him got us into just as much trouble so it's hard to say whether it was an asset or a liability.

There I go again talking about assets and liabilities. I'd promised myself that I'd never utter those words again, but here I am breaking that pledge in the first part of the story. You see, after Mother died—I like calling her "Mother" now, even though I never did while she was alive—anyway, after Mother died, I was stuck going with Dad on house calls to see his clients. We'd drive all around the county, picking up monthly premiums while Pop tried to sell poor, unsuspecting souls more needless life insurance. He loved to use the "assets and liabilities" angle whenever possible, especially, when he was losing their attention. It reminded me of Mother every time.

Only after begging him for several months did I finally convince him to let me stay at home by myself. Even though he was still skeptical, something in these tortured eyes of mine must have touched a sympathetic nerve in his soul. Maybe it was because I had my mother's eyes. Maybe he heard her in my voice, pleading for mercy. Either way, it was a defining moment in our relationship, as he'd come to realize that I was growing into manhood.

I'm sure a part of him was relieved, too. Since Mother had died, Dad spent every waking hour watching over me. A part of it was due to the accidental way in which she left us. She wasn't even supposed to go out that evening. If he hadn't already been three sheets to the wind on bourbon, it would have been him at the hospital that night instead of her. But being the loyal, caring wife that she was, always looking out for her husband's well-being, she told him to stay home as she ran into the next town to get him cigarettes.

When we got the call later that evening to come to the hospital immediately, everything changed. She'd been involved in an accident out on Route 1. That statement alone was a sure death sentence, and my dad knew it. The only wrecks that occurred on Route 1 between the small towns of Wingard and Bunsen Creek involved two cars colliding head-on going 60 miles an hour. On the drive over to the hospital, his hands wouldn't stop shaking. He could barely keep the car on the road. More than once, I had to reach over and straighten the wheel, because we were about to careen off the highway.

After the funeral, my dad never touched another drop of liquor or a cigarette again. Sadly, it was a drunk driver who'd crossed the double yellow line that put Mother in an early grave. Then to add insult to injury, the family of the other driver was one of Dad's clients. How ironic was it that he'd just sold them a huge policy upgrade a couple of months earlier, which assured Dad the title of Salesmen of the Year and, thus, the reason he was out celebrating that fateful night in the first place. And to top everything else off, we found out that Mother was pregnant. No, there wasn't a God in my father's eyes, only the devil in disguise.

Anyway, I digress.

That year, four people came into my life and changed it forever. Well, actually five including Sally, but, as I said, I'll explain that part later. I would have easily given up meeting them all for another few days with my mother. Of course, that wasn't going to happen, so I needed to count my blessings instead. Geez, now I'm starting to talk like her. Funny, how that sort of thing happens to you unexpectedly. I mean the talking like my mother part. I guess we all have those nurtured habits instilled in us as children that don't quite reveal themselves until the proper moment later in life. That must have been what my father heard in my voice that day he decided to let me stay home by myself.

Well, enough about my mother for now. Even though she was a big part of my life, she's not the only reason I'm here. Please just bear with me, because her memories are still very fresh in my mind, every day, and everywhere. Every time I look in the mirror, I see her face. Every night when I tuck myself into bed, I feel her kiss on my cheek. Every morning when I walk into the bathroom, her perfume lingers in the air. Every meal that I eat in the kitchen, I hear her singing at the stove.

That's what I liked the most about going over to T.J.'s house. His mom cooked every night, and the aromas coming out of that kitchen always reminded me of my mother. I could tell what they were having for dinner just by the smell coming down the street. When she asked one afternoon if I wanted to stay and eat, I didn't even hesitate to accept. Between the TV dinners and bologna sandwiches I was living off at home, any kind of cooked meal was a real treat. T.J.'s mom probably recognized that fact by the way I always circled back around and ended up in the kitchen when she was at the stove. Mothers have that kind of sixth sense when it comes to those things. At the time, I didn't even realize I was doing it.

Either way, T.J. and I soon became good friends. He was a few inches taller than the rest of us, and the best athlete when it came to sports. I remember teaching him how to shoot a bow and arrow when we first met. It was one of the few things that I'd inherited from my mother. You see, she was the athlete in the family. She loved basketball, tennis, golf, archery…you name it. Dad, on the other hand, couldn't hit a target the size of Texas with a B-1 Bomber. Sure enough, within an hour, T.J. was hitting bull's eyes while I was still trying to keep my arrows out of the neighbor's yard. Two peas in a pod we were, you might say. He liked baseball, and I liked baseball. He liked Steve McQueen, and I liked Steve McQueen. He liked girls…well, hell, we all liked girls.

That brings me back to the subject of Sally Nack. Sally was the first person to befriend me that year at school. It's bad enough having to move to a new school but transferring halfway through the year makes you stand out like a pimple on a forehead. There were the usual smartasses giggling behind my back in class about the funny-looking shoes and haircut. Occasionally, someone would even try to trip me in the hallway. I didn't mind. My dad had sat me down and explained what would happen that first week of school before we'd even unpacked our suitcases. What he didn't cover or anticipate was that a girl, a beautiful girl at that, would come to my rescue. She was my knight in shining armor—with a ponytail.

The day it happened, I was waiting in line during gym for the next Four Square game. It's a game where you chalk off four squares and each person controls his area. If the ball bounces in your corner, you have to hit it back into another square before it hits the ground again. Simple enough—except when someone cheats. I'd always been a pretty quick learner, and it didn't take me long to figure out how to stay in the game.

Things were moving along just splendidly until an older kid named Billy Hightower and his three pals decided they wanted to hog the game for the rest of the period. He was the chief of police's son and made sure everyone knew it. I was in control of the serve and sent it to his little brother, Jerry. He patted it over to Bobby McIntosh, who served up a lob to Billy. It was a set-up if ever there was one. Billy grabbed hold of the ball, the biggest no-no in Four Square, and pounded it into my corner. The ball sailed ten feet into the air and fifteen feet out of the square before coming down on a group of girls sitting in a circle, gossiping on the sideline.

"You're out, fuzz-nuts," shouted Billy.

"You held the ball," I retorted.

"No, I didn't."

"No, he didn't," chimed in his cronies.

One thing led to another until Billy had had enough of the small talk. All it took was one shove and I was on the ground. After all, the big lug must've had thirty pounds on me, as it was. I quickly sprang up, ready to do battle, when Sally stepped in.

She came between the two of us. Then she looked up at Billy's washed-out eyebrows and tiny brown eyes and said, "Back off."

Billy jelly rolled his belly into her chest. "This ain't your fight, Blondie."

She didn't budge, almost like she was expecting it. I realized later on that it wasn't her first tussle with Billy the Bully. It wouldn't be her last either. "It is now, fat boy," she replied.

That was all it took. Billy grabbed her by the shoulders and was ready to toss her to the side like King Kong would an airplane when Sally belted him one in the stomach. It wasn't a random punch either. She knew exactly where to place it to do the most harm, and did she ever. Billy curled up and moaned like a cow. Sally just nodded to me and walked away, as innocent as a black widow that'd just kissed her husband goodbye for the last time.

The teacher heard his cries and came running over, asking what was the matter. Billy took one look at Sally, knowing good and well that admitting to being flattened by a girl would ruin his reputation forever, and just whimpered, "Food poisoning."

The teacher had him escorted over to the nurse's office where they filled him full of cod liver oil and ipecac syrup. Poor Billy spent the rest of the day vomiting breakfast and purging last night's dinner. All the while, the rest of his disciples gave Sally and me the stink eye every chance they got. She didn't mind it though. They had about as much guts to follow through on their threats as the Cubs had chances of winning the World Series that year.

The next morning, Billy cornered Sally against a wall near the bathroom and said that her days were numbered. I'm sure he said it to save face, but if the kid had had half a brain, he would have realized that a statement like that would eventually come back and bite him on the ass someday. Rumors of the threat made it back to me by lunchtime, so I had to set things straight with Sally.

I grabbed my lunch tray and nabbed the last seat across from her at the table. "Hey, I wanted to thank you for yesterday."

"No need. The jive turkey had it coming."

"I'm sure, but I could've handled it myself."

Sally turned and gazed into my eyes, searching from left to right, probably trying to see what was going on inside my head or something. At the time, I didn't realize what was happening to me as my hormones were just starting to kick in. Love was still a concept I'd only experienced in the words of Emily Brontë and the other authors we were forced to read in English class. All I know is that for the rest of the day, I couldn't get her out of my mind.

"I'm sure you could've, Newbie, but being that you're new and everything, I had a feeling the teacher would've sided with Billy. I wasn't about to let that happen."

Her answer made complete sense. And she was right. What teacher in the right frame of mind was going to expel Billy Hightower and not expect a speeding ticket the next day? Or maybe even worse, be carted off to jail for some minor infraction and then find their name in the newspaper the next morning. No, Sally was a sharp girl. She had more street smarts than an alley cat.

It took a few weeks for word to get back around to her older brother. She did all she could to contain him when he confronted her about it, but once Lonny's mind was made up, there wasn't much you could do but walk behind him with a shovel to clean up the mess he was about to make. He did pick the perfect setting to send a message to Billy and his gang. I don't know if Billy was just totally unaware that Sally had an older brother or just stupid enough to think that his dad's standing in the community would protect him. Either way, he'd sorely underestimated the wrath of Lonny Nack.

It was the Fourth of July weekend, and everyone was picnicking out at the Lakeview Leisure Club for the day. Situated a mile and a half outside the city limits, the Leisure Club was the most popular entertainment spot in the county. Motorboats raced around Bunsen Lake all afternoon with skiers performing death-defying twists on ropes and inner tubes, while others catapulted off the ski ramp situated in the middle of the water. The lake was just barely wide enough for a boat to circle around without slowing down. When you added on a water skier to the back, it was a completely different type of adventure. The tricky part was making the turn next to the dam without going over the edge. If you had an inexperienced boat driver, chances were that the skier would end up with a bird's-eye view of the whitewater bubbling up below the waterfall. If that wasn't enough to grab your attention, the occasional stump or log poking up from the bottom during drought season definitely would.

In most other places, this recreational water hole would have been abandoned long ago because of the dangers surrounding it. But after spending so much time and money building a clubhouse and pool with dues paid years in advance, the good people of Bunsen Creek were willing to look the other way. Of course, that's just a figure of speech as many of the members made a sport out of taking bets on which skier would veer closest to the drop-off.

The Shades of Blue was jamming near poolside and entertaining the swimmers with its own breed of rock and roll with a touch of soul. They had a black bass player in the band who sang lead named Leroy Washington. He had a voice so sweet and pure that even the birds stopped to listen when he opened his mouth. He was also one of the funniest people you'd ever meet. In front of a microphone, he could sweet-talk the old ladies onto the dance floor and keep the men chuckling at the bar.

His parents were the only racially integrated family in Kickapoo County. His father had grown up in Carbonville and secretly married a white girl from Wingard. That alone was enough to set off a few cross burnings in the neighborhood, but this was no ordinary girl, mind you. No, she was the mayor's daughter and, with that, came a few privileges. Unfortunately, those perks didn't extend to having an open invitation to swim at the Lakeview Leisure Club. Being a private club, they were allowed to pick and choose who they wanted as members. Normally, that just meant anyone with enough money to pay the dues, but when it came to black folks, well, that was a different story. That was also the reason why the band had set up outside the fence instead of near the pool. If that bothered Leroy, he didn't show it. This was a paying gig, and he didn't care if the women swarming around the stage giving him google-eyes were yellow, red, black, or white.

Fireworks were set to go off at nine, and the blankets were sprawled out, lining the banks of the lake like patches on a quilt. I had managed to sneak away from my father for a little while and was enjoying a pop with Sally down on the dock. As the sun set, families finished up the last few pieces of fried chicken while others stretched out and snuggled together waiting for that first aerial bomb to explode, signaling it was time for the show.

"Newbie, tell me about your mom."

"My mom? What's there to say? She grew up in Wingard and met my dad, who was from Bunsen Creek during high school. They were married right after graduating."

"Did she have any brothers or sisters?"

"Yeah, but they all moved away soon after her parents died. I guess they didn't have kids until they were really old, and, well, you know…they ended up dying shortly after my mother finished high school. Most of the family moved up to Chicago where the rest of my relatives are."

Sally picked up a rock and skipped it across the water. It skidded a good thirty feet before sinking. Then she stared straight ahead and said, "I miss my mother's laugh the most. She could bring a smile to anyone's face when she was in a good mood." She took a deep breath. "What do you remember most about your mom?"

I had to think about that one for a while. The memories were all still so fresh that nothing stood out. Images of her from my childhood toppled over each other as I tried to focus on one. To tell you the truth, I hadn't even gone through the normal stages of loss and grief that psychologists say you experience. I was still stuck in some kind of denial purgatory or "depurgannal" to use another term. Huh, I just made that one up. That sounds like one of those anti-depressant drugs they put whackos on. It was just so much easier to push those thoughts back into a cupboard buried deep in my mind and ignore them. I was more focused on the fact that Sally had just opened up and divulged such a personal revelation. I'd never had a moment like this with a girl before, and it felt awkward, yet comforting.

Then we heard a screeching sound coming from the top of the hill. "Testing, testing, one, two, three. Is this thing on?"

"That's Lonny," exclaimed Sally. "Let's go see what he's up to."

With that, we both ran up the hill to the pool area where the band was getting ready to start the next set. Lonny was on stage, slapping Leroy on the back and laughing. Then he walked up to the microphone and said, "You know, I learned how to play harmonica when I was in prison. That's where I met Leroy, too. I was there for… disturbing the peace, and he was there…I guess, for being black."

The drummer did a short roll off the snare, kick drum, and cymbal as the other band members chuckled. I looked into the rest of the crowd, and the only people laughing were other teenagers and a few hippies off to the side of the stage. Now that I think about it, the hippies pretty much giggled throughout the whole set. Leroy walked up to the other mic and said, "I guess it's a little too early in the day for that joke."

Lonny pulled his microphone off its stand and replied, "I'd say it's never too late to grow a conscience."

The guitar player whispered something into Leroy's ear. He cleared his throat. "Well Lonny, what are you going to play for us?"

"This is a little blues number called, 'Good Morning, Little Schoolgirl.' See if you boys can keep up with me."

And with that, Lonny placed a harmonica up to his mouth and started wailing. In an upbeat double-time rhythm, he blew some of the sweetest notes you'd ever heard while tapping his foot in time. After making it through a whole eight measures, Leroy, who'd been snapping his fingers along with the beat, moved up to the microphone and started singing, "Good morning little schoolgirl. Good morning little schoolgirl…"

Lonny jumped in with another rousing four bars of harmonica at the end of the first verse as the crowd started clapping along. The sound was so pure and simple. All it took was a man with a harmonica, a foot, and a voice. The two of them didn't miss a beat as Leroy sang the next verse, and Lonny belted out the second solo. By now, the drummer was keeping time on the high hat. Lonny nodded to the guitar player, who joined in with his own solo. Leroy softly started thumping along with the bass as the kick drum came in. Seamlessly, the whole band had eased into a full rhythm section.

People were dancing on the concrete deck and shuffling in the grass near the stage. With her back to me, Sally grabbed my arms, placed them around her stomach, and began boogying while standing in place. The music went on for another three or four minutes as they struggled to figure out how to end the song. Finally, Leroy raised his arm and brought it down swiftly on the backbeat. The band stopped simultaneously. Then he went into a flurry of improvisation, holding notes and weaving words up and down the scale so effortlessly. The band whipped out a few more chops, bringing everything to a blazing climax.

As the audience swarmed the stage, cheering them on, Lonny spotted something in the crowd and jumped off the platform. This evidently caught Leroy by surprise, but he quickly recovered and yelled, "Give it up for Lonny Nack." Lonny high-fived people right and left, as he quickly shuffled by. Just then, Billy Hightower barreled passed us with the rest of his gang. The look on his face said it all: He was running for his life.

When Lonny ran by us, Sally shouted, "Please don't do anything."

He just ignored her and kept going. Sally started after him, but I grabbed her arm. "There's nothing you can do. Whatever they get, they deserve. Let's go watch the fireworks." She could've easily gotten away and trotted off after him, but she didn't. She knew I was right.

Through the choruses of "oohs" and "ahs" rippling down the hillside that night, another spectacle was taking place up on the far side of the clubhouse. By the time the fireworks' grand finale had rolled around with the rockets' red glare, and bombs bursting in air, pudgy Billy Hightower found himself butt naked and tied to the flagpole with his underwear flapping in the wind at the top. Lying beside him were his compadres in crime hogtied and wrapped in a bow with their own sets of underwear stretched over their heads.

The line of cars heading home that evening each saluted the boys goodnight with a flicker of their headlights as they turned and drove out of the parking lot. I don't know why it took a good fifteen minutes before anyone realized that something was wrong with this picture: Maybe the drivers were distracted by their kids yelling and pointing out the backseat window, maybe they were too tired to stop and just wanted to get home, or maybe they were glad to see justice finally prevail. Either way, poor Billy Hightower never did recover from that one. He managed to quell most of the teasing from kids his own age, but, boy, did the adults have a field day with it. Even Officer Hightower couldn't write enough tickets to silence them.

Chapter Three

Sally and I became great friends during the next few years. In the beginning, I never could quite gather up enough courage to ask her to go steady or try to steal a kiss. It was one of those slow-cooking romances that needed to be stirred every once in a while, but never quite came to a boil. But did we ever come close. I suspected that she was about as green around the gills as I was when it came to relationships.

That's where Skeeter came in and filled in the gaps, compliments of a stack of *Playboy* magazines he'd pulled out of his father's trashcan. He had a wealth of knowledge on the subject. Not only had he been to first, second, and third base, but if you got him in the right mood, he'd tell you about the home run he'd hit with the girl from upstate Illinois who'd come down to visit relatives one weekend. Yes, at the ripe old age of thirteen, Skeeter had blissfully spread his seed into the other sex's garden and was damn proud of it. At least, that's the story he gave us.

Of course, we didn't believe a word he said since none of us had ever met this mysterious girl, but we let him ramble on anyway. The guy did have a way with words though. With his slicked-back hair, long sideburns and gentle, disarming smile, he could spin a tale so outrageous yet so believable that you'd swear it must have happened. Then he'd deliver an unexpected punch line or joke at the perfect time that had you bending over with laughter. We'd let him strut around, gloating, from time to time just for the fun of it. Besides, none of us could top his list of achievements, so who were we to try and steal his thunder?

Yes, I learned a lot during those years in junior high. Most relationships were as shallow as a birdbath, with the exception of two: There was Sally, of course, but we always seemed to be going in different directions those first few years. Then there was Mary Makowski. I didn't even know Mary existed until one of my favorite teachers, Dr. Shelder, whispered a little too loudly under his breath, "Man, that girl's gonna break some hearts."

Dr. Arnold Shelder lived a few blocks over from my house. He was a tall, dark-haired man who liked to wear a tweed sport coat and scratch his balls while lecturing us about the finer points of modern science. There was a plaque on his wall next to a wooden paddle that said "Doctor of Philosophy," which would explain why he was teaching instead of practicing his profession. Some people said that he taught just to cover expenses while finishing a book he was writing for some big-name publishing house in New York. Others concluded from the way he ogled Miss Lenhart that he was madly in love with her and stuck around just hoping that one day, in one perfect setting, with one intimately revealing conversation, they'd become lovers.

Now anyone who'd ever had the pleasure of passing Miss Mya Lenhart in the hallway immediately understood which theory was true. Who wouldn't want to cuddle up with her instead of a typewriter? To every male in the student body, she was known as "Mya Glandhard." She was every teenage boy's dream girl: smart, sexy, and sweet. Students frantically moved around schedules in order to take one of her English classes. Some boys even went as far as flunking them repeatedly just for the pleasure of watching her write on the chalkboard year after year. Understanding that was enough to convince me that Dr. Shelder knew what he was talking about when it came to Mary Makowski.

Mary had a wiggle ten years older than her walk and more moves than a runway model. I knew she was way out of my league but that only made me want her more. My opportunity came a few days later due, in good part, to Dr. Shelder stepping in. He paired us together for a science project: dissecting a frog. Poor Mary didn't have the heart to touch the frog, let alone cut into it. We both knew that she'd flunk the class if she didn't participate, so with a few precise incisions and a couple of very thin stitches, I was able to make it look like she'd cut and quartered the frog like a birthday cake.

"Thank you, Newbie," was all she could say for the next few days. She said it in the classroom, she said it on the way home from school, and she said it in her bedroom after inviting me over for milk and cookies. It was the first and only time a plate of cookies went untouched in my presence, but boy, was it worth it. She was the best kisser by far in junior high, and I thought I'd hit pay dirt.

We continued to kiss and neck during the next few months and even had one of those favorite boyfriend/girlfriend songs that all love affairs are supposed to have. You know, that song zooming up the charts being played every half hour on the hour that is there every time you turn on the radio. Then, just because one or two lines from the lyrics happen to coincidentally relate to some event in your life, your significant other deems it "our song" for the rest of the relationship. Although Mary was quietly singing along with Roberta Flack's "The First Time Ever I Saw Your Face" when we slow danced down in Buzzard's dark basement, I was silently humming into her ear "Bang A Gong (Get It On)" by T. Rex. Unfortunately, she never got the message I was trying to send or just chose to ignore it. You see, the girl had morals and was saving herself. At least, that's the line I got every time I tried to round the bases with her. Now I knew what Dr. Shelder meant about her breaking hearts.

Yes, we snuggled, necked, French kissed, held hands, you name it. Every boring thing known to man was on her list, and all of the good ones were locked away in some imaginary chastity belt she had strapped to her waist. That was pretty hard to take, considering there was still enough spillover of free love going around from the whole '60s revolution. I had Skeeter bragging about his fling with the upstate gal, Rudy the Beer Man carting around vanloads of girls drinking Boone's Farm wine and defiantly waving their bras in the wind, couples at school getting caught in the boiler room with their shirts undone, the list goes on. So, as anyone else my age would've done, I did the expected: I lied.

I didn't quite come out and write it on a T-shirt or anything like that. It was usually one of those subtle don't-quite-answer-the-question type of responses that secured my place among my peers as a person who was "getting some." And since I didn't really come out and say we were doing it, Mary was okay with the charade. How that quite made sense, I'll never know. But, of course, nothing ever makes sense to a teenager when it comes to sex.

Anyway, I digress again.

With the longer days came another tradition started by my father back as far as I can remember: chores. First, there was cleaning the garage and setting any junk items out on the curb for pick up. Then there was trekking down the hillside behind our house and cutting down any overgrown vegetation. On the surface, this might've seemed like a lot of work, but I enjoyed every minute of it. The property lines for the row of houses on my block all bordered Bunsen Creek. Every one of them had a picturesque view of the trees and bushes tapering off down the rolling hills onto the valley floor where the river flowed.

You had to be careful where you stepped though. During the early 1900s, there were coal mining operations all up and down the slopes. European immigrants, from Poland to Hungary to Lithuania, ventured across the Atlantic to work in the mines. All it took was a letter or telegram from a relative stating that there were good-paying jobs waiting for them in America, and they were ready to leave everything behind.

After the mines closed, they were supposed to be filled in and returned to their original state. Sometimes that happened, but most of the times, the owners left town practically overnight, fleeing authorities and hiding behind a series of corporate loopholes. Therefore, the land sat barren and fallow for decades, with mineshafts flimsily covered up enough to be hidden from sight but not enough to weather the elements and time. The land did recover nicely as trees and bushes sprouted through the ashes, and water filled the lower lying pits, creating deep pools and eddies on the riverbanks.

During mushroom season, the place was crawling with hunters up and down the slopes searching for thinly veiled patches of tasty

Morels hiding in the undergrowth. Every spring after the rains, dozens combed the area for arrowheads. At other times, kids played in the creek, building floating vessels out of nutshells and racing them from one end of the stream to the other. The older children held hands and meandered along its banks, stealing a kiss when no one was looking. It was where my mother and father had met. They didn't call it "Bunsen Creek Valley" though. To them, it was forever known as "God's Country."

A very unexpected and strange incident happened that day while I was chopping away bushes and clearing brush down in the valley. Something that I've never been able to understand or even tried to explain to anyone else. Anyone hearing me describe that afternoon would have surely called the paddy wagon and carted me off to the loony bin without asking questions.

I saw my mother.

Not only did I see her, I talked with her. Now I know what you're thinking, so please don't even go there. I'm sure it was just an illusion or daydream of some kind. But at the time, it seemed so real, and, to be honest, I wanted it to be real.

It wasn't like she just came into view in front of me and started speaking. No, it began as a warm breeze blowing by so uncharacteristically strong that I stopped what I was doing and took notice. It almost felt as if someone was nudging me and saying, "Hey, over here." I dropped my machete and followed the path down to the creek. It was a bright, sunny day, and the light filtering through the trees reflected off leaves in ways that could play tricks on the mind. Every time the wind blew, glimmering images emerged and swayed back and forth through the branches. That's when she appeared.

She was wearing a green and yellow summer dress with her long hair up off her neck and tied in a knot. Both hands were behind her back until she smiled and bent down to pick a flower. Then her image went out of focus and vanished. I quickly ran over to the spot and shouted, "Mom"—"Mother" just didn't seem right to say at the time. I waited for a minute, and when she didn't reply, I turned to walk away. Before I could take my first step, a branch brushed my shoulder. Then I heard her. It was just a whisper submerged within the sound of the babbling brook, but I was sure I heard her say, "How are you, Ryan?"

It was strange hearing my birth name spoken, especially, since moving to Bunsen Creek. Even my father had resorted to calling me "Newbie" on most occasions. I was almost hoping that she'd called me by my nickname, because then I would've known I was imagining the whole thing. Now, I wasn't sure about anything.

"I'm okay." The words drifted off my lips. I waited again for the longest time but heard nothing. Just then, the sound of crunching leaves interrupted the silence. Behind me were footsteps, so I spun around as quickly as I could, hoping to catch a glimpse of her once more.

"Hold on there, Newbie. That's a good way to get yourself shot." It was Lonny carrying a rifle in one hand and two dead squirrels in the other.

"Holy crap, Lonny. You scared me half to death."

He took a long hard look at me while unfolding a pack of cigarettes from his shirtsleeve. Then he pulled one out, lit it, and inhaled deeply. He held it for a few seconds before exhaling and saying, "You look like you've seen a ghost."

The comment couldn't have been more spot-on. I lowered my head, half embarrassed and half lost for words. "Yeah, I think so."

Lonny raised one eyebrow and just took another drag off his cigarette. I'm certain he wasn't sure how to respond to that remark. He fumbled with the squirrels for a while and tied their tails into a knot. "There, that'll make it easier to carry."

I glanced at his rifle. "Old Man Tranchant know you're out here?"

"Old Man Tranchant can kiss my ass," he exclaimed. "No one should have the right to own that many acres of land, especially near the creek and all." He reached into his pocket and pulled out a rock. "Look at this arrowhead I found down by the water. You know, this could have very well been made by one of my ancestors. This land belongs to him about as much as it belongs to me. No matter what it says on a piece of paper."

"It is a special place," I replied.

"Damn straight it's a special place. This is Mother Nature at her best." Then he toned it down a bit. "At least Old Man Tranchant's heart is in the right place. Lord knows what would happen if somebody else gotta hold of this land."

I just nodded in agreement and pointed at the squirrels. "Is that dinner?"

"Yeah, sort of. This'll make a nice stew and that's about it."

"You play a pretty mean harmonica, you know."

He exhaled slowly. "You liked that, did ya?"

"Oh yeah. How long did it take you to get that good?"

"Seven months, three days, and four hours to be exact. That's how long I was up at St. Charles."

"I see." There was an awkward silence between us. I mean, what can you say after a comment like that? *"Gee, tell me all about your time in lock up. Was it fun? Did the guards let you play with the other kids or whip you to sleep every night?"*

Lonny could tell that the comment made me feel uneasy and asked, "You play?"

"No, not at all."

"Do you wanna play?"

"Heck yeah."

He pulled a Hohner Marine Band out of his pocket. "Here you go. It's yours."

I carefully took the harmonica with my right hand, thanked him, and twirled it from top to bottom. It had a small dent in the top and scratches everywhere, but it was still a beauty.

"The first thing you need to do is hold it in your left hand." Lonny turned the harmonica around and placed it correctly in my fingers. "Then just start blowing."

"But I don't know any notes."

"You don't have to, really. That's the beauty of the mouth harp. The notes on it are already part of a musical scale. You blow any of them, and you will be playing some kind of tune right off the bat."

"Yeah, but how do you know which ones to play?"

"That comes with practice, my friend. After a while, you'll get the hang of it and figure out where you should start and where to end. Everything in the middle is just gravy. Go ahead."

I slowly lifted the harmonica to my mouth and blew. A three-note C chord spit out between the brass reeds.

"Not bad. Now use your lips and tongue if you have to and try to play just one note."

"Do I blow in or out?"

"Well, that's a good question. That's where you and the mouth harp have to become one. Once you've learned all of the notes, it will tell you whether to blow in or out. It all depends on how you feel. If you're in a good mood, do more blowing out. But if you're a bit down and out, you know, maybe sitting in a cold, hard cell, sleeping on a thin cot next to some idiot named Butch, you might want to breathe in a bit more. You know, make sure you're still alive and all." He took the last drag off his cigarette, tossed it onto the ground, and added, "After a while, it'll all come naturally. And when you finally find your true voice, you'll be singing like a bird."

I nodded and just stared at the harmonica. I could only imagine how it must've saved his sanity while away at the correctional center. Being separated from your family at such a young age then having to learn how to get by and survive on your own must have been hard to deal with. Yet, by giving me the harmonica, I think he was somehow letting go of his past.

He seemed more chipper already as he slapped me on the back. "Well, I gotta go." Then he motioned to the hill and asked, "Mind if I cut through your backyard? Going all the way down the creek takes an extra fifteen minutes."

"No problem."

And with that, he was gone…and so was my mother.

Chapter Four

The flagpole incident set the tone for the next couple of months with Lonny. A part of him had been unleashed by his little escapade at the pool, leaving him uncensored and unsupervised from then on. His father couldn't control him, and the police seemed to be a little afraid of him. His weekly adventures circulated around town faster than a tornado in a toilet bowl, and within no time, the name Lonny Nack had become synonymous with legend.

First, there was the soda pop incident at the Grab-It-Here grocery store. Seven cases went missing one sweltering hot morning out of the back of the store and showed up at the baseball diamond around noon. Lonny was selling them for a dime a piece and sold out before anyone was able to put two and two together. He was also smart enough to collect all of the empty bottles and dispose of them before the ink on the police report had dried.

Next came reports that someone driving a beat-up truck with no license plates was filling up his gas tank at stations outside the county line and driving off without paying. The suspect always wore a baseball hat down over his eyes and never got out of the truck. In most cases, he would ask for a quart of oil from the attendants and take off as soon as they went inside the station. None of them ever got a good description of the guy because the sun was in their eyes as he drove off, but they were able to confirm that he did have a middle finger.

Week after week, the stories poured into Buck's Diner, making it around tables so fast that even the waitress couldn't keep them straight. And, boy, did the townsfolk have a field day with the chief of police. Every time he set foot in the place, someone would work into a conversation the line, "Whatcha gonna do about it, Chief?"

That line was about as welcomed as a fart in an elevator to ole Tony Hightower, and by the time August ended, he'd had enough of Lonny Nack. I guess Lonny somehow just figured that he wasn't really hurting anyone, so what was the harm? No blood, no foul, right? In his mind, he was more of a modern-day Robin Hood: stealing from the rich (meaning anyone he didn't know) and giving to the poor (meaning anyone he did know). Most businesses refused to bother with filing police reports. They knew that the less stink they made about it, the less chance a copycat would show up the next week.

There was even a rumor about Lonny robbing a bank upstate near Chicago with a vibrator in a paper bag. By the looks of his truck and wardrobe though, if he had, he definitely wasn't spending any of the loot on himself. At least that was the story Buzzard gave us when the subject came up in one of our sleepovers. He was running the soda fountain at his dad's diner part-time that summer. The gossip mill was churning out more stories about Lonny than it was ice cream. Old men would come in, order a coffee and a single scoop, then sit and talk for hours. They loved playing Monday morning quarterback, discussing what the police should've, would've, and could've done. Mothers would come in with their children and order root beer floats, then poke spoons at each other while exchanging samples of "did you hear this" or "did you hear that."

Buzzard always had a new story or two that he'd tell as we smoked Marlboro Lights and sipped on Blackberry Brandy. We, of course, smoked lights instead of regular because we were concerned about our health. He had a way with words that was beyond comparison when it came to delivery. Even the silver-tongued Skeeter couldn't slap together such big words and explosive adjectives into a sentence quite like Buzzard could. For the most part, we just let him talk. I mean, what else did we have to do in such a sleepy small town besides roam the streets and get into trouble? It was best to just sit and listen to a few new stories, sip on a drink or two while watching Johnny Carson on TV, and then go out and get into trouble.

Of course, sometimes the stories got lost in translation. I remember one exchange that sounded more like a "Who's on first?" skit than a conversation:

"Old man Rogers said Lonny drove a girl over to Indiana to the movies and knocked her up."

"Who in their right mind would get in the truck with him?"

"That's not what I heard at the Grab-It-Here. Mr. Sampson said Lonny knocked over a wooden statue of an Indian girl with his truck."

"You're all wrong, douchebags. Mrs. Pritchard told my mom that Lonny knocked an Indian out for yelling at his girlfriend with one punch, just like in the movies."

"Hey, watch your language, dick-wad."

"It's my mouth, and I'll haul coal out of it if I want to..."

I think you get the idea of what I'm talking about.

By the end of August, Lonny had perfected the art of raising hell with a reputation that followed him everywhere he went. People began to see less and less of him around town and when they did, it wasn't for long. He was that cymbal player in the back of an orchestra. The one rarely seen behind a curtain but always heard with a resounding crash at that pivotal moment. Bunsen Creek's own little version of Zorro or Batman.

Streaking was still in its infancy that summer, but we'd all heard about it or seen reports on TV. Usually, Bunsen Creek was about ten years behind New York or L.A. when it came to fads or new gadgets, but that was before Lonny came onto the scene.

As much as we'd tried to convince ourselves that he was all balls and no brain, those close to him knew better. I remember hanging out at Nick's Nacks one afternoon, playing pinball on one of the old machines that Joseph had rebuilt while listening to Sinatra on a vintage Rock-Ola jukebox. Lonny was sitting on a beanbag chair, sipping a glass of Tang and reading the *Wall Street Journal.* He shook his head and said something about the damn Arabs and how they were going to take over the world with their oil supply. I barely knew what an Arab was, let alone why that affected my oil supply. Every teacher at school also recognized that he was smarter than the average bear. That was, of course, when he actually went to class and did the work. I'd say that fact alone kept him out of more juvenile detention centers than anything else. Once a judge looked at his academic scores, he had no choice but to give the kid a second, third, and fourth chance. Besides, Lonny's dad needed him at the shop more than ever those days. Old age was catching up to Joseph Nack.

Sometime around the middle of August, a rumor started circulating around town that Lonny was going to streak right down the middle of the square in broad daylight. The words were enough to raise every God-fearing parent's pitchfork in town. There were sermons at church condemning such lewd acts of the flesh to the point that most children walked away believing that Adam and Eve must've been born in a set of robes. Storeowners feared the damage this could cause to the fine reputation of our small town, as if it were the equivalent of Mayberry, North Carolina, or Disneyland's Main Street USA.

Even the chief of police got into the action, creating a task force comprised of his sidekick, Frankie 'Fat' Ferny, and the neighboring Wingard police department. They drew up diagrams of the square, marking points of ingress and egress up and down Main Street, while labeling every landmark that could help with their capture. They even had a code name for the operation: "Operation Flash Gordon."

During the next few days, there were many false alarms. People would start gathering around the square based on a tip coming out of Hank's Oasis. When nothing happened a few minutes later, the crowds slowly dispersed, and everyone went back to their normal routine. Lonny, of course, was staked out nearby, watching every move. After witnessing the police springing into action within a minute's notice, he realized that he had to come up with a foolproof plan…and did he ever.

August finally dropped off the calendar, and Labor Day Weekend was upon us. Most of the people in the county were at the Labor Day parade that afternoon in Wingard. The high school band meandered through an extremely long, dissonant version of "Space Odyssey 2001" as the trumpet players fought for control of the sound over a couple of highly enthusiastic snare drummers. Onlookers cracked open cans of Budweiser while their children chased candy being thrown by fair queens from the back of convertibles. Makeshift floats propped up with chicken wire and tissue paper carried signs with slogans like "Support Local Union 624," while dragging empty cans on fishing wires in the road. Even the veterans on the floats throwing candy balanced their aim with a beer tightly secured in the other hand.

I guess I should stop here and devote a couple of paragraphs to clarifying that last observation. Wingard is a small, neighboring town of about three thousand people with roots going back to the 1800s. At the turn of the century, there were twenty-four coal mines operating throughout Kickapoo County, but during the roaring twenties, there were more than 137. Almost all roads from the mines led to Wingard's downtown. Therefore, in keeping with the entrepreneurial spirit, the city's mayor at the time decided that these miners needed to spend some of their hard-earned cash in Wingard before going home to their families at night.

An ordinance was passed that eliminated any restrictions on the number of saloons within city limits and made obtaining a liquor license easier than buying a pack of gum. Before long, Wingard boasted more taverns per population than any other town in America, and the residents were damn proud of it. It instilled a sense of pride rarely found in such a small eclectic community. I mean, where else could you walk into a bar and buy your priest a beer without feeling any guilt or need for salvation? I'm sure it violated a few passages of written scripture and generated enough Hail Marys to even make the Pope blush, but it worked for the good folks of Wingard. Although many taverns closed the same day the mines were boarded up, traditional habits were hard to change. So, still to this day, you can walk down any city block and wet your whistle in one of the fine establishments there until the sun comes up. Maybe that doesn't fully justify their relaxed attitude when it comes to drinking in public, but it's a start.

As the folks lined both sides of the street, cheering on fire trucks and waving flags, a rumor was spreading that Lonny was going to streak through the Bunsen Creek square that evening at 7 p.m. You could feel the level of excitement grow with every turned head. I found myself torn emotionally about the event. On one hand, I was glad that it was finally happening, yet, on the other hand, I was kind of hoping the electrifying sensation it had generated across the whole county would never end. It felt like Christmas Eve, morning, noon and night. As my dad and I drove back to Bunsen Creek after the parade, I silently paid homage to Lonny and all he'd done for the community. There was a part of me that wondered if this might be his final curtain call though. He'd all but certainly be caught and sent to jail for indecent exposure, disturbing the peace, or any other trumped up charge they could pin on him. It was the end to an era—and definitely an end to one kick-ass summer.

I told my father that I had to help Buzzard up at the café and took off on my Kawasaki motorcycle looking for Lonny that afternoon. Officer Hightower, who lived next door, was out mowing his yard as I gunned it and ran the stop sign on the corner. Within seconds, he jumped into his squad car and was chasing me down the street with his sirens blazing and lights flashing. I turned the corner, ducked down the alley, and then pulled into Mary Makowski's back yard. Hightower blew right by and didn't even notice me. Mary peeked out her window and just shook her head. When I saw Hightower circle back and pull into his driveway, I took off again.

There was a sense of urgency in my quest to find Lonny. I'm not quite sure why, but I felt it was my duty to warn him. There was also another part of me that just wanted to find out what was going through his mind. What was it that motivated him to do what he was about to do but kept others like me from even thinking about it? I felt like a reporter trying to interview Houdini just before he attempted his last, fatal stunt. Something was telling me that I might never get a chance to talk to him again.

I set out combing the streets of Bunsen Creek. City planners a century and a half ago had laid the streets out using a grapevine as a surveyor's chain. I don't know if the grapevine had a personal or symbolic meaning to them or not. I'd like to believe that it was their subtle way of saying to the rest of Illinois, "We're not like you." Who knows? Maybe I'm reading way too much into it. They could have just as easily forgotten to bring a ruler to the design meeting and ripped off a branch from a nearby grapevine to measure with.

The streets were quiet with a few children playing in their front yards and the occasional home mechanic working on a car in the driveway. Most adults were hard at work in their back yards, trying to forget about tomorrow morning when they'd have to head off to Carbonville and punch time clocks at General Motors and Hysters or cash registers at Sears and Montgomery Wards.

Much to my surprise, it didn't take long to find Lonny.

Sally was sitting on the front porch swing, chipping off white paint from the arm rail as I rode up. One look at the rest of the house and you could see where she'd systematically chopped off blotches of paint from other areas over time. I propped my bike up in the front yard and strutted up to the porch. Sally brushed away the dirt and powder from her hands and said, "About time you came by."

The comment caught me off guard. Was she talking about me coming by to find out about Lonny or just to see her? "Well, I've been busy."

"Doin' what?"

"I dunno, baseball, football, stuff around the house, you know."

She remained quiet for a few minutes, absorbing my words like a sponge soaks up water and then squeezing them back out in a way that seemed reasonable. "I guess so. Your team won the county tournament last weekend and all. Things have been busy around here, too."

She saw that I'd planted myself on the railing instead of choosing a seat on the swing next to her. That's when I realized what her first comment meant.

"Get over here and have a seat," she commanded. "Are you thirsty?"

As I ambled over to the swing, a light purple bruise peeked out in between the layers of makeup under her right eye. She quickly turned away after catching me staring a bit too long.

"No, I'm fine. I'm not thirsty."

"Okay. How was the parade?"

"You didn't go? It was fantastic. Somebody in Wingard has a son who's stationed out at Chanute Air Force base, and he flew over in a jet fighter. It was so loud that babies started crying and windows were rattling all up and down Route 1."

That brought a smile to Sally's face. "That's cool."

There was another long pause between us before she added, "I'm looking forward to going back to school. It should be fun."

The comment struck me as odd as no one was ever happy to return to school. I could only imagine that her feelings on the subject were connected to the black eye in some way. Instead of arguing and telling her how crazy she was, I just agreed. "I think so. I hope we get the same homeroom."

With that, she reached over and placed her delicate hand on top of mine. I flipped my hand over and lightly squeezed hers into my palm. All of a sudden, that sense of urgency to find Lonny had faded away. Soon, I lost track of time as we talked about everything from the dangers and benefits of smoking marijuana to how good the Buffaloes football team would be that year. I'd never dreamt that sitting with her would be so easy and enjoyable. Sure, I'd had conversations with other girls on far deeper subjects, but never had I enjoyed such an exchange as I did that day. It was obvious that she felt the same way, too.

She brought a transistor radio out from the house, and we listened to WLS's Labor Day weekend show for the next two hours. Between Cream's "Sunshine of Your Love" and Bread's "Make It With You," we explored every emotion and tackled every question about life, love, and death that afternoon. As I sat mesmerized by her tropical green eyes, the purple tint underneath faded into oblivion and, for a short while, we both were happier than we'd ever been. The rose bushes were in full bloom, capturing hints of apricots, berries, and apples and swirling them into the air. Even the rising mercury in the thermometer on the side of the porch couldn't ruin this moment.

I could've sat there forever had it not been for Lonny's pickup truck pulling in. The beat up old Chevy sped down the driveway and disappeared behind the barn out back before the next chorus of "Jumpin' Jack Flash" could play out. Sally gently removed her hand and placed it back on her lap. We sat quietly and swayed to the music for a few minutes, trying our best to hear what Lonny was up to in the house. We heard a chair slide across the floor in the kitchen and a few pieces of silverware rattling in the sink, but that was about it.

Ten minutes later, there was a voice coming through the screen window behind the swing, rising a little higher with each syllable, "What are ya doin', Sis?"

I turned around just in time to catch Lonny's wink and smile as he took another bite of a sandwich.

"I'm waiting for Newbie here to propose to me. We're gonna get married tomorrow."

We all had a good nervous laugh about that one. Sally's semi-morbid attempt to get a rise out of her brother didn't seem to be working, but it sure was making me a little anxious.

"Well that's just peachy. I'd be honored, Newbie, to have you as a brother-in-law. Just as long as you didn't mind having me as your brother-in-law."

"I'd be honored, too."

Lonny gulped down the last of his milk. "Well then it's settled. Welcome to the family. I guess I'd better go start making arrangements an' all, seeing that the wedding's gonna be tomorrow."

"Don't worry, Lonny. We're going to elope."

"Ah, very cool, Sis. That's just the way I'd do it if I was your age, too. No need to get the parents all bent out of shape over two underage kids marrying before they'd even reached puberty."

"Hey, now you're being downright silly," countered Sally.

"Yeah, I guess you're right. So are you going to live here or over at Newbie's? I'd vote for Newbie's since it's right next to the creek and all. By the way, if your dad ever wants to sell that property, let me know."

"How in the world could you ever afford to buy it, Lonny?"

"Oh, you never know. I have my ways."

Buzzard's bank robbery story was the first thing that came to my mind.

Since the whole marriage exchange had been diffused, I saw my chance to ask the question I'd been waiting to ask all day. "So Lonny, are you really gonna do it tonight?"

Sally whipped her head around and glared at me with a look teetering somewhere in between curiosity and disbelief. I'd forgotten that she hadn't been at the parade and probably wasn't even aware of the news.

"Yeah, you've heard right," answered Lonny. "I'd say it's time, eh? I've made a promise to my fans and I'm gonna keep it."

"They'll be waiting for you, Lonny," said Sally in a half whisper. "What do you think Pop is gonna do if they catch you? I mean, around here and all. He can't handle the shop like he used to."

Lonny thought about this statement for a minute before replying. You could sense the internal struggle he was having between honoring his commitment to family and satisfying that uncontrollable urge of being a teenager. He cleared his throat. "Yeah, well, there comes a time in your life where you either learn how to chirp like a cricket or howl like a wolf."

"What the heck does that mean?" she asked.

"It means that there are some people that walk around on two feet and others like me that run on all four." He looked up and pointed, "I think there's a full moon tonight so you know where I'll be. You and Pop can handle the store. And if that don't work out, well, you got your new husband here to help."

"That's not funny anymore, Lonny."

"Don't worry, Sis. I think I've come up with a plan that'll have ole Tony Hightower and his posse chasing their tails before the night is through."

And with that, Lonny disappeared into a smokescreen of wire mesh and wooden floors not to be seen or heard from the rest of the afternoon. What was it that motivated him to fear nothing? The thrill of the moment, no matter how cheaply obtained or easily lost seemed to be valued more than life itself. It was like mortality was just an afterthought to him.

I'd soon worn out my welcome and exchanged goodbyes with Sally. As I was walking to my bike, she ran up from the house and yelled for me to wait. Then she laid a kiss on my lips so soft and succulent that it made my knees wobble. Mary Makowski couldn't hold a blowtorch, let alone a candle to this girl when it came to puckering up. I stood there and enjoyed the moment for as long as possible. I couldn't care less if the neighbors were watching.

Finally, the salt from her tears dripped down between my lips, ending the innocence of our exchange. She didn't have to say anything to justify her actions, as it was all understood. I just brushed back her bangs and said, "I had a great time today. Let's do it again."

She nodded, lowered her head, and replied, "Me too."

Chapter Five

On the bike ride home, so many thoughts were going through my mind that I almost missed the turn rounding the block near my house. This encounter with Sally had emotionally overloaded my circuits leaving me running on reserve power. I didn't even notice Chief Hightower sitting on his porch when I pulled in and parked in the garage.

Before I could get the garage door shut, he was standing in the doorway. We'd never gotten along very well for a number of reasons. Apparently, he'd wanted to buy our house from the old owner, but the guy wouldn't sell it to him. After living next door, I could see why. His dog used to dig up our flowers on a regular basis, and Hightower just ignored our pleas to keep him chained up. So my father reciprocated by peeing on his lawn every night and killing the grass. Add to that Hightower's brat of a son using a riding lawnmower to block our driveway with piles of snow every chance he got, and you had the makings of a neighborhood feud.

"I should cart you off to jail right now, son," he growled.

I mumbled under my breath, "Don't you have anything better to do?"

Hightower shuffled across the concrete floor toward me and yelled, "What was that? You getting smart-alecky with me? Let me tell you, boy, I spent three years in Korea during the war and saw dozens of young punks like you get their heads blown off because they were so cocky and arrogant and thought that the rules didn't apply to them."

"Boy?" came a voice from inside the darkened garage. My father's silhouette was leaning against the wall looking like the High Plains Drifter with the sun to his back. He placed his hand over an imaginary pistol on his hip and added, "I haven't heard that term used in years. What's the problem here, Tony?"

"I caught your boy, I mean, son, racing up the street and running the stop sign on the corner."

"Oh, you mean that same stop sign you run every morning when heading off to work?"

Hightower's tongue and lips fumbled for a complete sentence. "Yeah, well, he's not even old enough…that doesn't mean…"

"…That doesn't mean what? Don't go trying to scare him to death over running a damn stop sign, Tony. For God's sake, it's not like he robbed a bank or something." There was a long pause as the veins on Hightower's neck bulged out like skinny little fingers rising up and choking off his will to continue the argument. He shot me a piercing glare and sized up the shadow in the doorway. Then my dad said, "I think you need to take a chill pill and just go back home. Are we done here?"

"I'll let it go this time." And with that, he disappeared.

"That was so cool, Pop." I said as I shut the garage door.

"Get in the house…and stay off that bike."

"But Pop…"

"It's hard enough raising you on my own now, son. Let's keep the law out of this. Besides, you don't even have a license yet."

I hung my head. "You're right."

He put his arm around me and lifted up my chin. "You're a good kid. In fact, the best kid a father could ask for: low maintenance and obedient…but just stupid enough to stand up to Johnny Law." Then he sighed and added, "I guess I'll take two out of three."

That afternoon, as we ate TV dinners and caught the rest of the Cubs game on WGN, I realized just how lucky I was to have my father. It didn't matter what the score was with the game or what was hidden under the gravy on my tray, just being there together was all that was important. It's those moments that build an eternal bond between father and son. Not hugs and kisses or even enlightening conversation. No, it just happens through assimilation and maybe even osmosis. Every time your father runs his hand through his hair, the way he uses a fork, the words he uses to begin a sentence and even in the way he stretches out on the couch are teaching moments. That's how a father and son bond. All of those little idiosyncrasies that we define as traits are passed down from one generation to the next just by the simple fact that the two of you are spending time together. It's in those moments that we understand where it is we come from and who we will become. It's in those moments that a boy learns how to be a man.

As the shadows stretched across the living room wall and Jack Brickhouse recapped the game with another *Tenth Inning* broadcast, my mind returned to Lonny. I needed to alert the boys quickly before anyone else made other plans. You see, even though there was a standing invitation to always hang out in Skeeter's Backroom, there was one major exception to the rule, and that was when girls were involved. When the porch light was on, everyone else was to be gone, because someone was trying to work his mojo inside with a member of the opposite sex. That, of course, rarely happened. Skeeter definitely was the biggest culprit, but sometimes I think he just switched it on to get a rise out of us. I had to make sure that everyone would be available on what could be the biggest night of the year. A few phone calls later, we were scheduled to meet up in an hour and prepare for an evening of entertainment featuring Lonny as the headliner.

Never in a million years did I expect that a simple confirmation over the phone would put into place a set of events so monumental for the town of Bunsen Creek that people would be talking about it for years to come. Maybe it was the alcohol that prompted neighbor after neighbor to send out the alert, or maybe it was just the merciless heat causing their brains to malfunction. All I knew was that by the time Skeeter, T.J., Buzzard, and I had walked up to the square to get a good seat for the show, there were spectators lined up twenty deep on each side of the road.

There were rows of pickup trucks squeezed into the City Bank's parking lot, with their tailgates down and foldable chairs firmly secured in the back. Little children were playing tag on the sidewalk as their parents powwowed in circles and discussed Lonny's options. High school and junior high kids had commandeered the area between stoplights on the east and west side of the street slowing traffic to a crawl. Most folks just detoured down the alley and took another route. Even Charlie Springer, the meanest old miser that'd ever set foot in town, had crept out of his tomb of a house to take part in the pageantry.

The manager of the Grab-It-Here grocery store, which was located on the west side of the square, was fervently trying to prevent any more customers from entering. The two employees working the checkout lanes were so overwhelmed with the volume and long lines that people just started throwing dollar bills on the counter instead of waiting to be rung up. Every apartment building window above the diner and hardware store was jammed with spectators leaning out and yelling to friends below. On the roof, the smoke from charcoal grills blasted the sweet smell of hamburgers and steaks into the crowd below. People drifted by like cartoon characters, uncontrollably following the scent and ending up in front of Buck's Diner only to find a line waiting for tables stretching halfway around the block. Several onlookers had neatly rearranged some of the chairs in Dukas's Clothing Store and lined them up in the display case window.

Colonel Remus P. Entwhistle marched down the sidewalk with his signature white Bible raised high in the air, preaching fire and brimstone while handing out tickets for discounted carwashes. He was the only person silly enough to wear a suit to the event, and, even though it was two sizes too small for his belly, he managed to keep it buttoned up. With his thick-lensed glasses and white cowboy hat, the pint-sized young salesman shouted scripture so fervently that it would've made a nun blush.

"The Lord is upon us tonight and witnessing this blasphemous spectacle. Repent now you sinners before it's too late." He'd stuff a coupon into someone's shirt pocket and whisper, "Fifty cents off any car wash Monday through Friday."

And, of course, as was expected, Officer Hightower was leaning on his squad car talking over strategy with Fat Ferny and the

Wingard cops. You could feel the bitterness and envy pouring out of him from across the street. He stood there with his hands firmly folded across his rock-solid biceps, ready to take down an army singlehandedly, while Ferny gripped the handle of his pistol, just itching to swing into action at a second's notice. Even Hightower's moustache was on edge. They had a car strategically placed on each side of the road, set to blast off the minute Lonny showed his face. Cars traveling down Main Street crept along slowly, rubbernecking the whole way as they passed the growing crowd. There were more people on the streets that night than what was counted for the whole town during the last census.

As 7 p.m. rolled around, the audience began to quiet down and secured their final position to watch the show. Several lookouts took turns standing on the curb, sizing up every truck or car that came into view. Someone had lowered the Labor Day parade banner that stretched across Main Street and turned it into a finish line ribbon. Leftover lights from last Christmas had been lit up in honor of the occasion. They stretched from one street pole to the other forming a huge X over the center of the road. The temperature had cooled off nicely to a pleasant seventy-eight degrees.

The biggest question on people's mind was how Lonny would arrive. Would he show up in the back of his pickup and strut his stuff or come by in someone else's vehicle, get out in the middle of the road, and run around the car a few times? No one particularly cared one way or another just as long as it did actually happen. By 7:30, people were beginning to wonder.

Choruses of "I need to go to the bathroom" and "I'm hungry" rose from the throng of whining toddlers trying to escape the clutches of their parents. Some high school kids had ducked down into the alley for a cigarette break. Even crusty old Charlie Springer started the slow crawl back into his cave. Hightower and Ferny were soaking up the glory with the other cops, patting each other on the back for a job well done, protecting the good citizens from this decadent menace.

"Let's go over there and see what's happening," said Skeeter. We crossed the road and nonchalantly weaved in between the masses until we were right behind the squad car.

"Well, I'd say it's another false alarm. The kid doesn't have it in him," boasted Ferny.

"Let's give him another five minutes. Then we start dispersing the crowd."

"Hey, Alistair Dukas is waving at you over there, Tony."

Hightower nodded and said, "Yeah, I need to go over and talk to him for a minute."

Suddenly, the scanner inside Hightower's car crackled and popped, "Car 46, we have a 10-50 reported near the county line on Mill Street Road. Three vehicles are said to be involved. All available cars are to report immediately."

Fat Ferny nearly fell over himself reaching for the microphone on the dash as he acknowledged the call. Then he shouted across the street to the Wingard cops, "Hey, did you hear that?"

"Yeah, we're on our way." The two officers jumped in the car, turned on their sirens and red lights, then headed north on Main Street.

"Get in the car, Frank. I'm driving," shouted Hightower. And with that, he threw the Ford Galaxy into drive and sped off down the street with his sound and light show a blazing.

"10-50, what's that?" asked T.J.

"Car wreck," I replied. All three of them locked eyes and held their breath. There was only one reason why I knew the answer to that question, and I tried my best not to conjure up any memories from that fateful night years ago.

Skeeter nonchalantly commented first. "Sorry, man. We didn't mean to go there."

None of them, of course, knew her personally, but it didn't matter. It was just out of respect. As the flashing lights disappeared down Mill Street and veered east out of town, a beat up, old pickup truck slowly turned south coming from the west. Something immediately caught my eye about this truck, but I couldn't quite pinpoint what it was until T.J. spoke up, "Look, that truck has its lights off."

Just about that time, two headlights clicked on and the truck starting gaining speed. "It's him," I whispered.

"It's him," shouted Buzzard as he turned to the person on his side and added, "Lonny Nack's coming up the street."

The news spread like melted butter across the square, and by the time Lonny's truck was halfway up the block, people were cheering him on. "Go Lonny go, go Lonny go…" Parents helped their children clap in time with the chant as teenagers raised their fists in the air. Even Charlie Springer stopped and took notice.

There was a lone driver in the cab, sporting a tank cap with flaps, a pair of sunglasses and a bushy fake moustache. The disguise was right out of a pulp-fiction spy thriller. The truck crept into the square, barely breathing exhaust as it inched along. There wasn't another car in sight. Everyone kept chanting, "Lonny, Lonny, Lonny…" until their voices grew hoarse.

As the cheering died down, Alice Cooper's "Eighteen" rose out of the truck's stereo 8-track player. When the truck reached the stoplight, it turned red. The driver cranked up the volume and allowed every decibel of distortion to fill all four corners of the newly formed civic arena. From the bed of the truck, Lonny's head appeared, igniting a roaring response from his audience. Alice was near the end of the first verse and ready to blast into the chorus when Lonny jumped up buck-naked. His body was dry humping the glass on the front cab with both arms flexing a new set of tattoos into the air. His tight buttocks swayed to the music in Chippendales' fashion, disappointing no one.

People were going bonkers. Toddlers, teenagers, parents, grandparents, you name it, were all shouting and cheering him on. Ladies from the Methodist Church Sewing Club, boys from the local Jaycees, even Alistair Dukas, standing out in front of his clothing store, was getting into the action. As the chorus wound down sliding into the second verse and the light turned green, Lonny smoothly gyrated around, step after step, until he was completely facing the audience. The first thing people noticed was the Richard Nixon mask he was wearing. Disturbing but yet funny, it combined the paradoxical plight of everything that was wrong with the country with everything that was right. Something about a muscular built naked man grooving to the rhythm of Alice Cooper with a fifty-year-old face made you want to puke and laugh at the same time. Then people started to notice something else peculiar about his anatomy. Between his legs, swinging like a chimp on a vine, was a fourteen-inch penis. It wasn't your typical John Holmes penis. No siree, this was the Famous Mr. Ed and then some.

"Holy Mary!" cried Skeeter as he stared mesmerized and embarrassed simultaneously.

"Wow! Now that's a tally-whacker," added Buzzard.

"It can't be real," I concluded after knowing what Lonny was capable of doing with a rubber snake.

"If it is, he's just scared the piss out of every girl in the county."

And that he did. The women from the Methodist Sewing Club were screaming in disbelief and stepping over themselves trying to escape the view. Parents were covering their children's eyes and turning away. Alistair Dukas ducked inside his store and started turning off the lights. Charlie Springer, on the other hand, was grinning from ear to ear.

A few teenage girls stepped up to the truck for a closer examination as the vehicle slowly proceeded across the intersection. Undoubtedly, what had started out as a social event was now transforming into an educational field trip. Some of them couldn't keep from tripping over their mouths, while others just smiled and boogied to the music, winking whenever Lonny's eyes crossed their path. Still, most of the crowd just laughed. It may have been a nervous laugh for those single men watching him set the bar so high sexually, but still they were laughing.

The show went on for another minute or so until a car horn honked and blinked its lights on the north side of the square. I don't think anyone had realized up until then that they'd shut off traffic going north, south, east and west by pouring out into the streets for a closer look. Lonny glanced around at the headlights and pounded the hood of the cab. That was his signal to skedaddle out of town, and that's exactly what the driver did.

People hung around for a few more minutes but then started finding their way back to their cars and homes. They'd witnessed more excitement that night than some residents had experienced in a decade. The phone lines were buzzing all through the night as the conversations moved indoors. The four of us hung out at the light post and watched the crowd disperse. We knew this banner night would forever hang in the halls of every house in town, and we wanted to wrap ourselves in it as tightly as possible.

When all that was left were a few barflies and storeowners, Skeeter said, "Well, boys, let's call it a night."

As we made our way across the road, the Bunsen Creek's police car came racing up Main Street with its lights on but sirens off and swerved into the parking lot in front of Dukas's. Hightower tapped on the car horn, and Alistair soon emerged from the store. He had a package wrapped in white paper under his arm. When he reached the car window, he handed it to Hightower and shook his hand.

"Did you see that?" I asked.

"Yeah, what the heck was that?" cried T.J.

"Maybe it was a payoff of some kind," added Buzzard.

"Don't get yourself all worked up, boys," replied Skeeter. "There is something fishy going on with that package but not what you think."

"What do you mean?"

"I mean, it *is* fish. Dukas buys fish off Bobby McIntosh's father and cuts them up out back of his store."

"Why the heck would he do that?"

"Hell, I don't know. I guess he likes fresh fish—and doesn't like fishing. I've seen him out back a dozen times cutting them up. And boy, does it ever stink back there."

"He's already the richest man in town," I said. "Why would he cut them up himself?"

"Now that you say it, I've smelled it before too," added Buzzard. "I just didn't know where it came from."

T.J. leaned against the light pole and said, "Well, go figure."

As Alistair recapped Lonny's little caper to both officers, Hightower's hands strangled the steering wheel. Fat Ferny pounded the dashboard as he radioed the Wingard squad car. There was no wreck out on Mill Street Road. They'd been duped once again and, worst of all, in front of the whole town.

The four of us stood in the shadows near the alleyway and watched. They talked for the longest time. Soon, the Wingard cop car showed up and waved them on out of the limelight, motioning to continue south out of town. Alistair patted Hightower's shoulder and fumbled for his keys. All three cars sped off and weren't seen the rest of the night.

As far as that goes, Lonny wasn't seen for the rest of the year… until New Year's Eve.

Chapter Six

The night that Lonny did reappear was almost as memorable as the streaking incident. We were at my home away from home, Skeeter's Backroom. "The Backroom," as we'd christened it, was just what it sounded like: a room in the back of his house. His colossal two-story home had been built before the Civil War and was originally designed to be a small inn. Legend had it that it once housed a budding Senator from Illinois named Lincoln. At the turn of the century, the property was converted into a regular house where generations of Skeeter's relatives lived together comfortably. Over the years, most of them moved out or passed away leaving just his parents living on the top level while his grandmother occupied the front part of the ground floor. That left the back area, with its wrap around colonial-styled porch, full basement, and back room conveniently at our disposal. Add onto that the fact that his grandmother was nearly deaf meant we could be as loud and obnoxious as we wanted without bothering anyone.

We were listening to WLS on the radio while Jimmy Saint James counted down the top 100 songs of the year. "Alone Again, Naturally" was ringing out of the two gigantic JBL speakers strategically placed on both sides of the couch. As Gilbert serenaded us on piano, memories of my mother wandered in between verses. What would she think about my new set of friends? What corny words of wisdom would she offer up as I told her that I was spending New Year's Eve with them, knowing good and well that we'd be tossing back a few beers and throwing up Blackberry Brandy before the stroke of midnight? Jimmy Saint James interrupted the last few bars with, "And that's the number two song of the year, folks." He cued up a corny radio jingle and added, "I'll be back right after this commercial break with the number one song of 1972."

"How can that be? If that's not the number one song, then what the hell is?"

T.J. was sprawled out on the couch with a *Playboy* magazine draped over his face trying to take nap. I heard him say, in a sarcastic muffle, "Is that a rhetorical question?"

"Rhetorical? I'm surprised you even know what that means," I replied.

"Hey, dipshit, I take English class."

"Yeah, but you never take your eyes off the teacher."

"Well then, she must have 'rhetorical' tattooed on her ass somewhere."

Skeeter's neighbor, Rudy, had taken our five bucks to buy beer an hour earlier, and we were still waiting for him to return. Skeeter went outside in the bitter cold to look for him. He'd delayed going out as long as possible, but we were damn thirsty and bitching up a storm. Besides, it was his neighbor anyway, not ours. That winter had been merciless and downright freezing. With record snowfall and wind chill factors off the charts, you had to be awful thirsty to venture outside. That's when Skeeter came bursting in out of breath and shouted, "You won't believe what just happened. Lonny Nack's in jail!"

"What?" T.J. and I shouted in unison.

This statement even got Buzzard's attention while he was fixated on watching *The Tonight Show* with Johnny Carson. Once Buzzard got into his "zone," you might as well have been talking to the wall, because he wasn't listening. Even though this little trait had pissed us off more than once during those years in school, I was sure it would pay off in dividends for him later in life. I could already picture him in surgery up at Kickapoo County Hospital playing tic-tac-toe on some patient's chest while rearranging their coronary arteries.

He turned down the volume and emphatically repeated what we'd just said: "What!"

"Lonny Nack. The cops just caught him at Hank's Oasis," said Skeeter as he peeled off the layers protecting him from the cold and rubbed his hands in front of the space heater.

"No shit. Rudy just told me. That's why it took him so long. Said four cops went into Hank's, two through the front door and two from the back. Lonny was sitting at the bar when they called out his name and said they wanted to question him down at the jail. He picked up a chair and rammed it into Fat Ferny and then reached for Hightower's gun. That's when the Wingard cop came up from behind and clobbered him over the head with a club. They had to carry him out on a stretcher—handcuffed."

"Whoa, that's heavy."

All I could think about at that moment was how Sally and her father would take the news. Since Lonny's disappearance, the Nack family had all but sequestered themselves from the rest of the town. The chief of police came by the shop once a week and asked if they'd been in contact with him. They even questioned Sally, pumping her full of righteous rhetoric and talk of civic duty. I felt guilty myself for not talking to her more about the whole situation, but, being a guy and all, it wasn't my strongest suit.

And then to make matters even worse, I hear Roberta Flack singing, "The first time, ever I saw your face…"

"No freaking way this is the number one song. Jimmy Saint James, you suck!"

The news about Lonny's arrest made the rounds that holiday faster than Santa Claus could deliver presents. It was even there in black and white on the front page of the local section of the *Carbonville News*. Sally called one morning and asked if Lonny could borrow a suit for the hearing. He'd outgrown the one he used the last time he was in court before a judge. Since T.J. was the only one of us near Lonny's size, I put in a call to him and asked to borrow one of his sport coats. He reluctantly agreed. I wrapped myself in layers of wool then trekked through the snow over to T.J.'s place.

He was standing at the door with a jacket and pants wrapped neatly inside a garment bag. When I reached up to grab it, he pulled it away and said, "This is my best suit, so make sure I get it back."

"Don't worry, dude. You'll get it back as soon as the trial is over."

When I finally made it over to Sally's, she was still dressed in her pajamas. Her father had closed the store for the holiday and was off visiting his sister over in Indiana. All of the blinds were pulled from the night before but every light in the house was on. I guess it made her feel safe.

"Here's the suit you asked for. I hope it fits." I hung it over the door and sat in the chair next to her.

"Thanks, Newbie. I'm sure we can make it work." She was curled up on the couch with her knees to her shoulders and just sipped from a cup.

"If there's anything else you need, just ask."

She stared into her cup and sighed. "There's nothing you can do. There's nothing anyone can do. What's done is done."

Her statement struck me as odd coming from the ultimate optimist. "What's been done?"

When her sultry eyes teared up and met mine, I did something that I've never done before. Something so strange and indecent that just writing it down makes me blush with embarrassment: I cuddled and listened. By doing practically nothing, her emotional floodgate opened up and guided me downstream through an unforeseen passageway of fears and dreams. I passed through her deepest and darkest secrets with such ease that I wasn't sure if what I was hearing was real. I had no idea that this side of the opposite sex even existed, and, to tell you the truth, wasn't sure whether I wanted to know. As I held her in my arms, she sobbed and eventually filled me in on the conversation she'd had with her father that morning.

Lonny was up at the Carbonville courthouse awaiting charges of assault on a police officer and destruction of government property. Apparently, he woke up in the back of the police car on the way to jail and proceeded to rip the seats apart with his teeth. Little did he know that, and I quote, "Such a willful depredation of leather and foam is considered to be a felony offense in the state of Illinois." Lonny had been smart enough to use a prosthetic penis during the streaking incident, which meant he couldn't be charged for indecent exposure. Why he'd gone crazy in the bar was still a bit of a mystery to everyone. Maybe it had something to do with a bottle of tequila and his ex-girlfriend showing up earlier that evening. It was all immaterial at this point though. There wasn't going to be a plea bargain any time soon, and bail was set so high that the chances of him getting out were less than winning the lottery.

Bernard Bates was a pudgy, thirty-year-old lawyer who'd graduated law school in the lower portion of his class and failed the bar examine four times before passing. That meant that all of the bigger law firms wouldn't return his calls, so he settled for a job as the Assistant State's Attorney. The pay was horrible but the benefits were good. There was a nice medical and dental plan, a decent 401K, paid holidays and steady hours. That meant, Bardy, as those at the courthouse knew him, had plenty of time to pursue his other passion: drinking.

Dressed in a wrinkled suit and bow tie, he frequented the halls of the courthouse, handling the dirty work for his boss and letting the newly elected State's Attorney take all the credit. His double chin and receding hairline made him look much older than he really was. Add to that a peculiar habit of burping up every other word that came out of his mouth, and it was easy to conclude that the man was a born loser. But that couldn't have been any further from the truth. He had what some people would say is the best asset a person could ever be blessed with: good luck.

No matter how hard he tried to fail at life, some miraculous event always intervened and saved the day. When he was just seven years old, he tried to splash water from a mud puddle onto a girl with his bicycle but lost control. Just as his bike went crashing into the bushes, a bolt of lightning struck the mud puddle that he was aiming for. Even though he was a pitiful excuse for a student in high school, he was accepted into one of the better universities in the state because the clerk transposed every "D" into a "B" on his transcripts. During a drinking binge in Las Vegas, he lost every penny to his name. Then, on a whim, pulled the lever of a slot machine while leaving the hotel and hit the jackpot. The list goes on…

Fortunately, he kept most of the drinking to after hours and the occasional long lunch. Most judges frowned upon alcohol belching sidebars in the courtroom, so he needed to do everything possible to stay on their good side. He knew which side his bread was buttered on too, so when a case involving a suspect who'd assaulted a cop and destroyed state property came across his desk, the smart thing was to go for the maximum sentence.

Sally tossed the morning newspaper on the floor, rubbed her eyes and said, "I'm afraid that he's going away…for a very long time."

"But he's not even eighteen yet, is he?"

"It doesn't matter. There's a new State's Attorney in office, and he'll want to make an example of him 'cause of all the other stuff they say he's done."

Her words settled like cement on a sidewalk. Nothing I said could argue with those facts. I discovered a whole other side to Lonny that day. Sally talked for hours about the selfless brother who took groceries over to the neighbors every week because they were too old to walk to the store themselves. How he would practically give away items in the shop when he knew the people buying them were dirt poor. She told me how he would help her with her homework instead of doing his own just so she could get an A in class. There were funny stories about how he would sweep the floor by putting her hamsters in socks and letting them shuffle across the room. She talked about how he'd sworn to protect her from Billy Hightower no matter what the cost.

Images of Sally's black eye from months before came to mind. "Sally, I got your back. If you ever need anything for any reason, just call me. And if you can't get a hold of me, call Skeeter or T.J. or Buzzard. We all have your back." I gently rubbed my fingers on her cheek and added, "Do you understand?" She smiled and nodded. I later updated the boys about the promise I'd made to Sally. They were more than willing to step up to the job.

When Lonny's case went to trial, Joseph Nack did everything he could to keep his son out of prison. He faced an uphill battle though, because every prosecutor in the county had lined up to take a shot at his son. Even with the help of his sister, who worked in a courthouse in nearby Indiana, they didn't stand a chance. After weeks of negotiations, pleading for leniency, and filing for a continuation, the sentence came down hard and cruel. Lonny was to spend the next three years at the Vandalia State Prison, stamping license plates and looking over his shoulder.

The rest of freshman year was uneventful and downright boring. We later referred to it as "The Year of Starvation." It wasn't just because of all the harassment we received from upperclassmen. No, that got old shortly after Billy and his gang took the shortest kid in our class and stuffed him in a trashcan upside down during P.E. class. They faced the wrath of Coach Collins for that one, and by the time they'd served out their punishment a week later doing an extra hour of running every night and getting up at five o'clock in the morning to cook and serve breakfast to the teaching staff, they were over the whole concept of hazing.

What really christened that year as "The Year of Starvation" was the fact that almost every freshman girl had forgotten that we existed. I guess it's sort of a rite of passage for women as they do mature much earlier than guys. Who could blame them though? Given the choice between an awkward, underdeveloped freshman and an upperclassman with a car and letterman jacket, which one would you choose? Skeeter didn't even bother replacing the light bulb on the backroom porch when it burnt out. What was the point?

Still, it hurt like hell, especially, when my precious Sally started riding around with the starting tailback on the football team. I put on my best poker face and tried to act like it didn't bother me, but it did. The worst part was not knowing if she was serious with him or just star struck.

Skeeter's father was the only person who could explain this phenomenon in a way that made us feel better about what was happening to us. Gus Willoughby was a truck driver who spent three to four days at a time away on the road. This, of course, made hanging out in the Backroom that much easier, but even when he was home, we felt welcomed. He and his wife, Francis, were the happiest couple I'd ever met. Even Walt Disney couldn't manufacture that level of joy. It was such a contrast from my own home life, even though I loved my father to death. He'd done his best to make our lives normal, but there was only so much one person could do.

That's why I loved hanging out at Skeeter's house. The minute that eighteen wheeler pulled into the back lot, there was magic in the air. Gus always stopped by to check on us before going upstairs. He'd sit and just shoot the shit about whatever was going on. He was no taller than five foot six with a potbelly that grew another notch on his belt every time I saw it. "Any good tool deserves a good tool shed over it," he'd say when you got him talking about sex and the size of his belly. Best of all, he had his own special charm about getting his point across that never came away preachy but always made us smile.

"Boys," he said, "let me tell you a little bit about dating women a lot younger than you. There was this old man who took his young girlfriend into a jewelry store one day to buy a ring. When the jeweler showed him a $5,000 ring, the old man said, 'No, no, no, I'd like to see something more special.' So, the jeweler went in the back and came out with a $50,000 ring and the old man said, 'I'll take it.' The young woman's eyes lit up as she squeezed his hand. 'How are you going to pay for it?' asked the jeweler. 'I'll write you a check. You can call the bank on Monday to verify the funds, and then I'll come by and pick up the ring.' Well, on Monday the jeweler called the man and said, 'There's no money in your account.' The old man said, 'I know, but let me tell you about my weekend!'"

I can still hear Gus chuckling over that story…and he had a hundred of them just like it for every occasion.

Over the next few months, T.J. and Skeeter both grew five inches taller. Buzzard and I added almost three inches, which put us at the same height as anyone in Billy's little gang. All of a sudden, Billy the Bully looked more like Billy the Blubber Boy since the only thing that expanded on him was his waistline.

With every inch in height we gained came another level of fearlessness. There wasn't a wooden paddle or principal's office around that could slow us down. I guess every boy growing up feels invulnerable to a certain point. That intrinsic quality seems to surface right around the same time that whiskers appear on your chin. As summer approached, we were ready for anything and cockier than the King of Spades.

When the balmy and hot summer nights were too much to tolerate indoors, we'd pack up the tent and take off camping at the dam. We spent many a night sitting around the campfire telling stories about how we were going to save the world from itself when we grew up.

"Someday I'm going to own a video company that only shoots movies with girls and big boobs," Skeeter said.

"Someday I'm going to make a hard on pill that combats the effects of a saltpeter," boasted Buzzard.

"Someday I'm going to invent a damn music player that doesn't loop every fifteen minutes," cried T.J. as he tossed a Three Dog Night 8-track aside.

Yes, we came up with all the great ideas between swigs of Mountain Dew and bites of peanut butter and jelly sandwiches. Unfortunately, that's as far as it ever went. We tackled deeper subjects, too, like the meaning of life and why Mary Makowski wouldn't put out.

"What's up with her curly bleached-out hair, I mean the carpet definitely can't be matching the drapes, if you know what I mean."

"I think she's rebelling against the whole sixties movement," stated Skeeter.

"Too much religion and not enough wine," chimed in Buzzard.

"Religion," I said. "What about the universe? I mean, what's on the outside of it and then on the outside of that?"

Buzzard continued my train of thought. "And think about what came before the universe started. You'd think that there had to be something before there was nothing."

"If you had a choice between hopping on a spaceship with aliens and going away for the rest of your life or staying here on earth, what would you do?" questioned T.J.

"That's it," I exclaimed. "Maybe Mary's an alien and can't have sex. That would explain a lot."

Skeeter just winked and boasted, "Maybe she just hasn't met the right guy."

The conversations would go on for hours just like that. The more we talked, the less sense it made. We weren't quite running on all fours yet, but we were definitely learning to crawl. The other great part of camping outside was stargazing. We'd plop a blanket down in an open field and just lie there for hours. That's when our true souls were unhinged and allowed to fly.

"When I finish college, I'm out of here. I don't know where, but anywhere's gotta be better than this place."

"Oh, I don't know. It's not so bad here. You got family and people you know. What makes you think it's going to be greener on the other side?"

The debates would ramble on throughout the night. Sometimes we'd stay up talking until dawn as long as there was a fire burning. Other times, the cricket noises could be just as soothing as ocean waves and put us right to sleep.

One time, I got up early to take a piss and noticed a light coming from the tree line below the dam. Everyone else was still asleep, so I decided to investigate. There was nobody in sight, and the morning chorus of birds had not yet taken their positions. It's funny how a void of sound can sometimes be more disturbing than a crowded street corner. We seemed to be programmed to absorb the noises around us: nature's own version of serotonin. That soundless morning should have been warning enough for me to wake everyone else up to go investigate, but I didn't.

I cautiously sauntered up to the tree line along the river. If ever there was a place to be alone with nature, this was it. As I neared the dam, the rushing sound of water pouring over its edge broke the silence. Pools of foaming white swirls dotted the basin like catacombs, burying the aquatic debris deep underneath the surface. Some branches and leaves emerged farther downstream where they were granted a second chance to float again. Unfortunately, the manmade garbage always survived that voyage and ended up wedged into the banks nearby.

I followed the river away from the dam and headed for the light. There was a radio in the distance yawning out a Hank Williams favorite. I heard someone humming along, "Yodel-lay-he-who, yodel-lay-he-who…yew-who." As I followed the ridge around the next bend, there was Dante Alagori down on the shore.

Back in the '50s, Danny Alagori, as he was known then, was married and lived in a house way off the road at the north end of town. It was buried in a wooded refuge of trees and bushes. One night, his house caught on fire while he was away, shopping downtown for groceries. When he arrived, screams were coming from a second story window. The fire truck hadn't gotten there yet, so Danny ran in and tried to save his wife. By the time he'd made it up the stairs, the house was engulfed in flames, and she'd jumped out of the window to her death. He dragged her away from the fire, her clothes still smoldering and just held her in his arms until the ambulance showed up.

As the firemen doused the fire with water, a set of blue flames shot out of the basement, followed by an explosion that was heard for miles. Most people around town knew that he had an illegal still in there since he'd been bootlegging moonshine on the side. After the fire, there wasn't any evidence left to tie the still to the cause of the fire. It was only his word against the word of onlookers who'd seen the flames, therefore, he never stood trial. I guess the townsfolk decided to administer their own brand of justice and nicknamed him Dante from that day forward. It didn't take long before every kid in town was chanting "Dante, Dante" as he passed by. After a few months of taunting and putting him through his own personal hell, he finally snapped and started chasing kids down the street the minute they opened their mouths. If he got close enough to you during the chase, you'd hear him growl, "I'll kill you, you little bastard." Fortunately, his old legs gave out long before he ever actually caught anyone.

Dante had a fishing pole propped up on a forked branch that'd been buried in the sandy gravel. He looked as happy as can be, humming along and whittling away a stick into what appeared to be a spatula. There was a small fire burning behind him with a skillet frying up four fillets of fish.

When he turned around and noticed me, both of our worlds froze in time. By now, the flowing river had gobbled up the roar of the waterfall. He squinted hard, sizing me up and trying to determine if I was one of the kids who'd teased him in the past. His knife was ready for combat as the morning chill still held a tight grip on the urge for either one of us to make a move. A burn scar stretched from the bottom of his neck to underneath his ear. He wore a large, puffy conductor's hat that shielded most of it from sight. No doubt, it was from the fire incident. I helplessly stood there like a bale of hay, waiting for the cold steel end of a pitchfork to determine my next move. The standoff went on for what seemed like hours, although I'm sure it was just seconds.

Finally, he stooped down with his newly carved spatula and turned each fillet over in the skillet. Apparently, he was more concerned about breakfast than seeking revenge. I just watched as the pan sizzled and shot back droplets of water from the greasy surface. His eyes were fixated on the spatula even though I sensed that his peripheral vision was still honed in on every breath I was taking. Then, he stood back up, and asked, "You hungry?"

Hungry? I don't think there was a single cell in my body that wasn't overloaded with adrenaline at that moment. You could've jammed a lobster tail and a fork full of steak into my mouth, and I'm sure my brain would've still told me to run instead of chew.

"Hey, you deaf?" he shouted.

I watched as he returned his knife to its holster and scooped out the fillets onto a two by four. He sat down on a log and motioned me to join him. I felt my body oblige as I meandered down the hillside. Before I knew it, I was standing next to the bank while he lifted off a piece of steaming white flesh with his fingers and put it in his mouth.

"Go on. Have a seat." He scraped one of the fillets onto another two by four and put it on a log sitting beside me. "The name's Danny. What's yours?"

"Newbie Johnson," I mumbled as I sat down and dissected the fish. I poked at it every which way possible before placing a portion in my mouth. "Ummm! That's delicious."

Danny laughed. "I thought you'd like it. It's my own secret recipe."

"Wow," I added as I devoured the rest.

"Go on. Take another. I feel lucky today. I think they'll be more where that came from."

"What kind of fish is it?"

"Catfish, straight from the river." About that time, his pole jumped out of the holder and bounced up and down as it twirled around. "What'd I say? Here we go again."

He gripped the pole and navigated the bobber from left to right with just the right amount of tension while slowly reeling in the line.

As a two-pound catfish burst above the surface, flapping its tail in defiance, he yelled, "Grab the net."

He skillfully glided the fish across the water and into the net with one swoop. Then he carefully picked it up while lecturing, "You gotta be careful with these here catfish. Grab 'em from the bottom like this and get under the fins or else they'll sting ya like a bee." He removed the hook and inserted a stringer line through the mouth and out the gills. Then he tossed the line back in the water. "There we go." I noticed another scar on top of his hand. The lifeless skin glistened in the morning sun, which was now sifting through the tree line. His long-sleeve shirt hid the rest of his arm. We sat back down and finished eating the other fillets when he reached under the log, and pulled out a can of Pabst Blue Ribbon. "Wanna beer?"

"No, thank you. I'm fine."

He popped off the top and took a swig. "Ahhh," he sighed. "So Newbie, I haven't seen you around town before. You new to the area?"

"I moved here a couple of years ago with my dad. We live down at the end of Seminary Street next to Officer Hightower's house."

"Oh, I see." I wasn't sure if his reply was referring to the fact that I didn't mention a mother or that I lived next to the chief of police until he said, "That was your mother in the car wreck out on Route 1 a few years ago, wasn't it?"

I lowered my head. "Yeah."

"Car burned up, right?"

All I could do was nod. That one sentence was all it took to change the whole dynamic of our conversation. We'd made a connection on a very personal level through the tragedies in our lives without even uttering another word. As the sun peeked out from behind the tree line, I thought I saw a figure move on the other side of the river. Just as before, the light glistened off the leaves creating a silhouette of a woman in a dress.

I began to call out when he added, "Sorry about your loss." Then he flipped up his collar covering the burn scar on his neck and asked, "What are you doing down here so early in the morning?"

"We're camping over on the other side of the cove. I saw your light and…"

"That's a good place to camp. I prefer downstream a bit. Not as many cars racing by in the middle of the night. There's always some hotshot spinning his tires in the parking lot around here or cutting across the cornfield trying to take the shortcut over the old deserted bridge. Idiot kids. If they'd just walk across that death trap, they'd see that it's covered with trees and crumbling concrete. You'd have to be a pretty good driver to make it through that mess."

"I know what you mean."

He pulled out his knife and dipped it into the river. "I think I'll cut this one up too. You know how to fillet a catfish?"

"No, but I'd better get back up there. The other guys are probably waking up wondering where I'm at."

"Suit yourself. It's been a pleasure."

"Me too. Thanks for breakfast." And with that, I climbed back up to the ridge and walked over to the campsite. For some reason, I decided not to share my encounter with the other guys. I don't know if it had something to do with the fact that they wouldn't believe me, or that I didn't want to ruin Dante's reputation.

When I entered the clearing, the other guys were up running around the tent yelling at a group of cats that had invaded our camp. The wild felines had ripped a hole in a bag of food and left a trail of Slim Jims all over the ground. "Get out of here you bastards," cried T.J. as he chased one of them under the picnic table.

"What a nightmare," moaned Buzzard as he picked up a shoe that had been marked with urine by a gray tabby. "This shoe is toast." He tossed it into the fire and asked, "Where have you been, Newbie?"

"Chill out, dude. I had to take a piss."

"I wish you would've peed in a circle around the campsite to keep these creepy kitty crawlers away," added Skeeter.

"Ha! 'Kitty crawlers,' I like that," chuckled T.J.

"Well, for a buck two-ninety-eight, I'll sell you one."

"For a buck-two-ninety-eight minus five, I'll take one."

"Jesus, Buzzard, now the whole campsite smells like piss smoke," I added as I wrapped a bandana around my face.

"No kidding," came a deep, low shout from the trail. "None of you boys potty trained?"

A man dangling a cigarette on the edge of the most smart-ass looking smirk stood before us. It was the father of Bobby McIntosh, Billy Hightower's best friend. Both Bobby and his father were carrying a fishing pole, a half dozen fish on a stringer, and a tackle box. They also had on matching camouflage jackets. I just wanted to go up and slap Mr. McIntosh in the face but, considering he was six foot four in height, I probably would have been lucky to swat the bottom of his disheveled long beard.

"Yeah, which one of you peed your pants?" chuckled Bobby as his father patted him on the back.

"Why don't you go eff yourself, Bobby?" whispered Skeeter.

"What was that, sonny?" growled Mr. McIntosh.

Without hesitation, T.J. barked back, "He said why don't you mind your own business?"

Nobody moved. T.J.'s fists were clenched as he stiffened his body, ready to do battle. I'd never seen him so angry. Buzzard and I traded glances as if we were trying to signal each other which person we'd take out first. Skeeter dropped a stick into the smoldering fire and brushed off his hands.

If it hadn't been for the two wild cats that curled around Bobby and his father's legs and then jumped up for the line of fish in his hand, I'm not sure what would've happened next. Their meows and hisses were enough to ease the tension as Mr. McIntosh said, "Let's get out of here. We don't have time for these young punks." And with that, they moved on up the trail and out of sight.

When the last cat had been chased off, Skeeter grabbed a sleeping bag and said, "What do you say we blow this taco stand?"

"Definitely."

Sally and I started to grow closer again by our sophomore year and, although we were never officially dating, neither one of us seemed to have any desire to see other people. Our relationship had blossomed into one of epic proportions, just like the books Miss Glandhard made us read in class. It had the devotion of Heathcliff for Catherine without the missed opportunities or tortured yearnings. It had surpassed Romeo and Juliet in passion but without the suicidal tendencies. It encompassed Tarzan and Jane's animalistic desires with the dramatic fervor of Sir Lancelot and Guinevere, but without the suspicious king getting in the way.

My father had been spending more time on the road with work and all that summer. Since Mother's death, his sales numbers had gone down tremendously, so he was forced to expand his territory to the surrounding counties. I could tell that his heart wasn't in the job any longer, but he accepted the additional responsibilities like a good soldier. This, of course, meant that there were many a nights when I was home alone. Things being what they were, it was only natural for a couple of hormonal teenagers to finally give in to temptation and exploit the situation.

Sally just happened to find her way into my bedroom one evening after cooking us a wonderful meal of spaghetti and meatballs. She loved Cat Stevens and saw a couple of his albums sitting on a chair in the corner of my room. What Sally didn't know was that these weren't my records. Buzzard had built up quite a collection of vinyl using the money he'd earned working in his father's diner. Every once in a while, he'd let me borrow a few albums, and I always returned them promptly. That is, with the exception of Cat Stevens. I don't know why I kept them, but I did. I think it had something to do with the way Stevens and I seemed to connect through his lyrics and music. When I was listening to him sing, I was always in a better place.

I sometimes found myself playing "Father and Son" repeatedly late at night with the headphones on and the lights off. It struck a nerve with me. Not just because I'd been avoiding that conversation with my own father, but because of the way he sang it. There was something about the deep, low voice at the beginning of the song, the father pleading for his son to heed his advice and then progressing into this high-pitched wail from the son begging his father to listen. Very few songs can get under your skin like that, and for me, this was one of them.

We both lay on the bed in my dimly lit room and sang along with every hit song on the *Teaser And The Firecat* album. With the black light reflecting off posters of the Beatles, Hendrix and Rolling

Stones, our hearts melded into one. Then I put on *Tea For The Tillerman*, which didn't have as many recognizable songs but still had a haunting personality of its own. By the time "Father and Son" came on, a sensation of warmness and serenity had brushed over my whole body. It made me feel so peaceful that I turned to Sally and kissed her on the cheek. She, in turn, slowly leaned over and kissed me on the lips. I lay there motionless as she softly stroked my face with her hand and kissed me again. It was just as gentle as the first one.

The acoustic guitar strummed in time with our heartbeats as I lifted up on my side and brushed back her hair. She closed her eyes and lay on her back, beckoning me to continue. Slowly my hand combed through her thick blonde hair, lightly touching her scalp as my fingers made their way down to her neck. Soon I was caressing the open area of her chest just above her cleavage. As I went to unbutton her blouse, a tear dripped down her cheek and onto my pillow.

"Sally, are you okay?"

She turned her head away and began to sob as the last note of the piano and vocal chorus faded away. The tonearm slid toward the center of the turntable leaving us both vulnerable to the awkward silence that followed. Over and over the needle jumped around on the vinyl, continuously skipping and popping dissonance out of the speakers. The aggravating rhythm was like a nudge on my shoulder telling me that I needed to venture further into this conversation. She was on her side now and trying hard not to be heard. I reached over and turned off the record player. Then I placed my hand on her hip and said, "Hey, I'm sorry. I didn't mean to overstep my boundaries."

Her head shook back and forth, as she wiped her eyes clean. "It's not you, Newbie. It's me."

There it was, that dreaded saying—the kiss of death to any relationship. More confused and almost to the point of anger, I asked, "What do you mean? I thought you…"

She swiftly turned on her back and said, "No, it's not like that. I didn't mean it to sound that bad." Her hand glided across my chest as she tried to smile. "It's just that I…I mean, I just can't do this."

I sat there for a while wondering where I'd gone wrong. Was I too fast, maybe too rough? My mind wandered into that forbidden territory of dreaded self-trepidation as I began to question everything I'd done. How could I have misinterpreted the signs so badly?

Sally could tell that she'd rattled my cage and leaned over to kiss me once again. Then she buried her head into my chest and tried to hold back the tears as she spoke. "I need to tell you something, but you have to promise that you'll never say anything to anyone else."

"Of course."

"No, I really mean you have to promise, especially promise me that you'll never tell Lonny."

"You have my word, Sally."

She reached up and squeezed me tightly for a moment. Then she slowly released her grip and said, "I know you saw the black eye I had last summer on the front porch, and I could tell you wanted to ask me about it but didn't."

At that moment, a light bulb went off. What an idiot I was for selfishly thinking that *I* was the problem instead of realizing that this poor girl might need to deal with her own set of demons. In a remorseful tone, I said, "I was too afraid to ask."

"I'm glad you didn't, because, at the time, I don't think I could've handled it."

"Well, can you now?"

She gazed into my eyes. "Yeah, but I'm not sure that you can."

Her comment was so unexpected. Images of blood, fists, and bodies being dragged in the dirt raced through my mind. I was definitely venturing out of my comfort zone here, but it was too late to turn back. I just had to know.

"Try me."

She inhaled deeply and let it out slowly. I could tell she was having trouble searching for the right words to start with. Several times, she opened her mouth, but nothing came out. Then she said, "That Friday night during Labor Day weekend, I was walking home from the diner. Daddy and Lonny were out of town picking up some furniture over in Indiana, so I went up town to eat dinner. About halfway home, a couple of boys started following me. I didn't think nothing of it until they started walking real fast. When I saw that,

I sped up and cut across the parking lot over by the grain elevator. That's when I saw the other boy waiting for me."

I reached out for her hand, and she squeezed mine tightly as she continued. "It was Billy and his gang. I walked right into their trap. I got in a few good punches before…"

She began to cry again, so I cut her off, held her close and said, "You don't have to say any more, I understand." We sat there in silence for what seemed like forever as I absorbed this revelation. Every emotion from anger to empathy to outrage poured out of my body as I tried to keep my composure. Finding words to fit the occasion was impossible.

"Newbie, I don't know if I'll ever be normal again. I mean, you know, be able to do what you wanted to do tonight."

"That's not important. Making this right is what's important." At that moment, I could've strangled him with my bare hands.

Sally grabbed a hold of my sleeve and said, "No, no one can find out, especially Lonny. He'd kill Billy and his friends for sure. Then I'd lose him forever. Promise me again that you won't say anything to anybody."

There was a look of fear in Sally's eyes. Where there should've been vengeance, I only saw concern. She'd somehow mentally made peace with herself and moved on as best as she could. The physical part was obviously far from over, but half the battle had already been won. It takes a special person to have that kind of courage, and, at that moment, I couldn't have loved her any more.

Chapter Seven

After her revelation in my bedroom that night, Sally grew distant. We continued to see each other, but less and less over time. Losing her brother's help at the store had taken a toll on the family. With her father's declining health, she had to work more hours in the shop. On top of all of this, I'd taken a part-time job at Dukas's Store.

Alistair Dukas was a New York transplant with an entrepreneurial spirit who loved a deal. When the building next door went up for sale, he snatched it before the realtor could get a sign in the window. He hired me to help him remodel and prepare the building to become a discount store. He was going to call it "Dukas's Discount Den" at first, but, thankfully, his wife intervened and insisted on "Dukas's Emporium." I spent the next few months painting and hammering after school while Alistair unpacked everything from imported leather couches to stainless steel toasters. He'd sunk a fortune into the place, and it was obvious by the way his wife came in with a stack of invoices and slammed them on the desk that he was rolling the dice on this business venture. His bushy moustache would curl up and his shoulders collapse under the weight of her interrogations.

Most of the time, he was a cordial boss who treated me fairly. Other times, usually soon after his wife left the store, he was a cold-hearted tyrant. He'd yell at me for not reusing packing materials to build displays and scream when I left a light on in the warehouse. The worst times were after Charlie Springer came by and repeatedly accused him of coaxing city hall into taking his cats away. I could handle the fits between visits from his wife. I could even handle his demeanor after crusty old Charlie gave him hell, but what really got under my skin were some of the other shady things that went on after dark. In fact, there were many times when I almost walked out and never came back. In order to save a buck or two, he'd switch out knock-off copies of items and resell them as brand names. They'd arrive in boxes that had been addressed in magic marker. Sometimes, there were boxes inside of boxes.

Most of the return addresses didn't even have a place of business listed on them, just a Chicago zip code and a P.O. box number. When they did have names, they were always derivatives of his family's like The Virgin Air Company, Angiben Acquisitions, and The Allistania Corporation. He did his best to hide them from me by opening the packages after I'd left for the evening. Still, there was only one dumpster out back, and I'd spent enough time moving boxes around in it to see everything. I didn't dare ask him about it. I'm sure he would have fired me on the spot, and I was sorely in need of the cash.

Ever since Mother died and Pop's sales figures dropped, cash had been tight. Up until then, the whole concept of money and what it was used for was still a bit elusive. Normally, all I had to do was ask my father for some, and he gave it to me. I didn't really know what it meant to go without until the one day when I needed it the most. The basketball coach had insinuated that anyone who wanted to play ball that year was going to have to buy a pair of Converse shoes. He even had the local Converse rep come in and give us a presentation on the difference between having the best basketball shoe on your foot and the worst. I must admit, it was convincing. If it meant spending twice what normal basketball shoes cost, then so be it.

Poor Pop just looked past me, staring out into a world that had come and gone, and said, "I don't have the money, son. You'll have to do without." I couldn't bear to see him like that, so I marched down to the square and started knocking on doors. Timing, being the essential building block to any successful endeavor, was picture perfect when I walked into Dukas's store.

The only good thing about visits from Alistair's wife was that she always brought along her daughter, Angie. Angie was a year younger than me with dark brown hair and eyes. She hadn't quite come into womanhood yet, but all the signs were there that she was going to blossom into one colorful flower. The first clue was her mother, Virginia. Although there was an aura of haughtiness that followed her everywhere, the woman had more curves than the Indianapolis Speedway. When she spoke, you didn't hear the spitefulness in her voice. No, you just saw the beauty in her delivery. Alistair was your typical-looking businessman with dark black hair, a huge snout, and bushy eyebrows. Angie, fortunately, didn't have any of those attributes. She was the spitting image of her mother right down to the long eyelashes and delicate olive skin.

I nodded to her and came down from the ladder as the door shut in Alistair's office. "How you doing?"

"Very well, thank you. So, you're the new hire, huh?"

"Yeah, they call me Newbie."

"I'm Angie. How do you like working for my dad?"

"He's alright," I replied as I gazed into the office window and tried to ignore the shouting coming from within. "Most of the time."

She chuckled. "Same thing at home."

Angie was sitting on a box, which was precariously lodged with a dozen other cartons stacked against the wall. When she shuffled around, it set off a mini avalanche. I lunged for her and covered her body as the mountain of cardboard tumbled down. Fortunately, they were all empty, and it sounded more dangerous than they felt. When it was over, my arms were around her on the floor, and my nose was buried into the back of her head. The scent of herbal shampoo and musk oil temporarily overwhelmed me, triggering a bout of erotic emotions that I didn't know existed. I quickly recovered and pushed the boxes away as her parents came rushing out of the office.

"Good heavens, what's going on out here?" demanded Mr. Dukas.

"Angie, my baby. Are you alright?" cried Virginia as they both ran over.

"I'm fine, Mother. Thanks to Newbie." As I pulled her up, it was as if my hand was holding petals from a budding flower, so soft and velvety. Our eyes met while her mother squeezed her tightly and brushed off the dust. It was brief and subtle, but there all the same, and I could tell just by the way she smiled back that we'd made a connection.

"You two should be going," said Alistair. "We'll continue talking at home."

And with that, they were gone.

The next life lesson came the following year when T.J.'s mother was admitted to the hospital with breast cancer. The prognosis was not very encouraging, as the symptoms had come well after the damage had already been done. We all stayed by her side during those weeks as she slowly deteriorated. I brought her soup and reminisced about the great meals she'd made me over the years. Her husband had to keep working in order to pay the doctor's bills since affording such a luxury like health insurance was nearly impossible for an independent contractor.

One night, I stopped by, and Skeeter's mom was sitting next to T.J. beside Mrs. Bowen's bed. I started to excuse myself when they asked me to stay.

"Come have a seat, Newbie."

Mrs. Bowen scooted up on the pillow and said, "Yes, come sit with us."

I didn't know what to say. After a long pause, I asked, "How are you feeling today, Mrs. Bowen?"

"Oh, Newbie, not too well."

The two women somberly smiled and wiped back a few tears. T.J. lowered his head and stared at the floor. It was apparent that they'd already had this conversation and I could feel the tension in the air.

"Don't worry. You'll be fine in a few weeks."

T.J. stormed out of the room without saying a word. I began to go after him when Skeeter's mom reached out and placed her hand on my arm. "Sometimes there's nothing you can do. You just have to place your faith in God and his will and hope for the best. Do you know what I'm saying? I'm going to be there for T.J. just like I'm there for Skeeter...and you, if you ever need me."

"That's assuming there is a God," I whispered. No sooner, than I'd said it did I regret it. It was a knee-jerk reaction, and I wasn't quite sure where it had come from. I quickly added, "I didn't mean that."

"I know, it's your father speaking there," replied Mrs. Bowen. "I've heard him say that a dozen times since the accident. You and he are very similar in many ways, but I do see your mother in you a lot. I mean, look at your eyes and nose, that same cute little nose. I bet you have her demeanor too: confident and compassionate."

Skeeter's mom rubbed my arm and said, "You're still young and learning. When you get out on your own and start thinking for yourself, then you'll come to your own conclusion about God and all. We won't ever judge you for that. Just like we'll always respect the wishes of a dying woman."

For the longest time, I just sat there speechless. Now I understood why T.J. had left so abruptly. They knew what was inevitably going to happen and had made peace with themselves and the world around them. They weren't still in a state of denial like Mr. Bowen and T.J. would be up until the end. I could only be so lucky to have that same kind of courage when my time came.

The walk home from the cemetery on that frosty, barren winter day chilled a part of my soul. Once again, a funeral confirmed that life was unfair and there wasn't a damn thing anyone could do about it. Well, to a certain extent. That night in Skeeter's Backroom, we toasted to T.J.'s mom and washed away a few layers of childhood innocence.

"Toss me another beer," yelled Buzzard as he navigated the AM dial onto 890. I pulled up the dumbwaiter from the basement and snatched a couple of Budweisers out of a cooler.

The dumbwaiter dropped down into what had become known as "The Hole." It was nothing more than a huge circular bowl of concrete with a set of doors. In the early days, servants would prepare meals in the basement and load them up on the dumbwaiter where they were lifted from one floor to another. Fortunately, most of the shaft had been boarded up, and the dumbwaiter now only traveled from the basement to the Backroom. This device had saved our butts more than once over the years. Very few people knew about it, so we were able to use it to sneak out of the Backroom into the basement and out the side door on many occasions without being caught. And to top things off, its prime location underground kept our beer cold long after the ice had melted in the cooler.

Between sips of beer, we hummed along with tunes from Sly and the Family Stone, Bob Dylan and Grand Funk Railroad. "Turn it up," cried Skeeter as King Harvest's "Dancing in the Moonlight" blasted from the radio.

"Now you're cooking, Jimmy," I yelled at the DJ residing somewhere at the end of that sound wave.

"Thanks, Newbie, for not returning my damn suit," scolded T.J. "I had to wear one of my dad's old ones at the funeral."

"Sorry, it's still at the dry cleaners in Carbonville. Besides, you looked fine."

"Yeah, well when am I gonna get it back?"

"You'll get it back. For Christ sake, Lonny's still in prison. What do you want me to do, drive up to Vandalia and ask him where it is?"

"I thought you just said it was at the dry cleaners?"

Skeeter tried to steer the conversation away from T.J.'s sports coat by saying, "A toast, to your mother."

We all raised our beer cans and clanged them together shouting, "To your mother." The saying stuck with us long after that, like an esoteric secret handshake. Not that it had any hidden meaning or anything. It was more or less our way of saying to each other, "Thank God, we're still alive."

"Ahhh," moaned Skeeter as he downed the last swig. "So fellas, what's on the agenda for tonight? We have to make this one count."

"Oh, I don't know," said T.J. "I'm not sure I'm up for celebrating."

"Who said anything about celebrating? I'm talking about getting out and seeing the world."

Buzzard pulled back the curtain on the window and exclaimed, "It's freakin' cold out."

"Precisely," I said. "Perfect weather for ice skating down at the dam."

"Wonderful idea, my friend. I think our skates are still in the basement." And with that, Skeeter wrapped himself around the dumbwaiter rope and disappeared into The Hole.

It takes at least two weeks of below-zero temperature for the cove at the dam to freeze up. That was never a problem in the Midwest. The locals were speculating that not only was there enough ice on the cove to skate over, but that it was thick enough for a person to cross the whole lake. Of course, no one was silly enough to test it.

The cove was a 50-foot wide and a 150-foot long area created for boats to load and unload into Bunsen Lake. When they'd constructed the dam decades ago, trapping the water from Bunsen Creek, the hope was that it would create a lake big enough to become the recreational hub of the county. Consequently, the Lakeview Leisure Club pool and clubhouse soon followed, drawing in visitors from all over the area. Unfortunately, the engineers were a little off on their calculations, leaving the town with a lake a little wider than a football field. On a good day, if the wind was in your favor, you could toss a rock from one side to the other without touching the water. Still, the cove made for a good hockey rink.

There's nothing quite like ice-skating in the middle of the night. The wind was usually nonexistent, and the stars and moon, combined with a single light pole positioned in the middle, reflected enough light down to cast a nice cozy glow over the whole area. The cove had been shoveled clean and now had two feet of snow surrounding a makeshift rink. In this rural version of street hockey, there were no masks, no shoulder pads, and no rules when it came to how hard someone could be checked into the snow bank. There was one rule about the puck though: at no time was it allowed to leave the ground. This rule was put in place for obvious reasons, as none of us wanted to walk around looking like a toothless Alfred E. Neuman, but there was another reason too. If the puck went sailing over the snow bank out onto the middle of the lake, then the game was over.

The only thing we had to keep our toes from freezing was a thermos full of hot chocolate and a small fire on the bank. With a transistor radio blaring and a full moon upon us, we played a game of epic proportions that night. Since we only had two people on each side, and both were needed to score points, we decided to narrow the goal to make it more interesting. One empty Folgers coffee can at each end was your target. Hit that and you scored.

As Buzzard stomped off through the snow to find more wood for the fire, an eerie sound rose from the forest. The farther he went into the brush, the louder the noises became. We skated over to the edge of the cove to investigate.

"Are those the same cats from the campsite?" I questioned.

"Yeah, but there's more of 'em. Feral cats. They've been out here for years," replied T.J. "I hear they came from Charlie Springer's house. You know, he used to be the mayor and was all high and mighty back in the day. He finally got voted out of office, partly due to Alistair Dukas backing the other candidate. After that, Charlie just let his house go and didn't give a damn about anything."

"No kidding," Skeeter said.

"Yeah, the cats stunk his place up so bad that the city eventually served Charlie papers and ordered him to remove them. Old man Springer got so mad that he dumped them out here. Dukas was furious, you know, being that he lives up there on the corner road and all. There's probably dozens of them out there now." T.J. continued.

"They've been feuding ever since, haven't they?" I asked.

"Definitely," replied T.J.

"Don't feed the cats, Buzzard," yelled Skeeter. "They'll follow you for life."

Buzzard appeared shortly after with an armful of branches. "Wow, that was scary—freaking cat city out there. They're everywhere."

The game went on for an hour or so with the score tied at four a piece when T.J. got carried away and reared off one of his famous chip shots to make it over Buzzard's stick. The puck went sailing over the snow bank in the cove and out onto a layer of smooth ice. Soon it disappeared into the darkness.

"Oh, for Christ's sakes. What did you go and do that for?"

"Sorry, it's just a habit."

"Habit, schmabbit. That was the only puck we have. Go get it."

"I ain't walking on that ice."

We all skated over to the edge of the cove. "What a bummer," I moaned.

When Skeeter arrived next to us, the ice cracked and air bubbles expanded in the thick layer below our feet. It scared the piss out of everyone and sent us racing over to the fire. As we plopped onto the snow, Buzzard asked, "Well, boys, so much for that. Any more hot chocolate left?"

We passed around the thermos, removed our gloves, and cozied up to the fire. Then a set of headlights flickered off the trees and water station next to us. Soon the silhouette of a truck came into view as the engine noise echoed down the road. It was going at least fifty miles an hour when it swerved off the road and skidded into the parking lot. As the tires squealed, sending the truck into a 360-degree spiral, gravel and snow spewed everywhere. We all covered our faces to keep from losing an eye, but that didn't stop us from stealing a peek as the truck slid up to our fire and stopped within spitting distance.

"Howdy, boys," rang through the air as the dust settled. The driver's door opened, spilling two empty beer bottles onto the ground, as a man in a T-shirt with a bottle in his hand emerged.

"It's Lonny Nack," whispered T.J.

"That it is." He took one last swig of the beer and tossed the empty into the bed of his truck, which was filled with sandbags. "You mind if I warm up at your fire?"

We all stumbled over each other, mumbling simultaneously and invited him in. Lonny had grown to at least six foot two in height with a set of cannon barreled biceps more daunting than aircraft carrier guns. His torso greeted the cold like it was a midsummer picnic, while the rest of us snuggled up deep into the body heat swirling around in our jackets. He pulled another bottle out of his pocket and twisted off the top. "Beer?" It didn't take us but a second to answer. He ran a hand through his G.I. haircut before pointing to the truck bed. "Help yourself. They're in the cooler."

As I walked by, he grabbed me and buffed the top of my head. "Well, I'll be. I almost didn't recognize you there."

"Same with you. You've, uh, been working out or something."

"Yeah, there's not much else to do in the Pen but pump iron and read...and play the mouth harp. You still playing?"

"Yeah, I'm getting pretty good," I replied.

"Well, I do have to hear you play sometime. We'll have to get together and jam."

"That would be cool."

As we stood around the fire, drinking beer, trying not to shiver and seem pathetic in front of a coatless man, Lonny asked, "So who the hell are these friends of yours, Newbie?"

One by one, they rattled off their nicknames:

"I'm T.J. Bowen."

"Skeeter Willoughby here."

"I'm Buzzard Buckner."

Lonny just grinned. "What the hell is this, a biker convention?" We all chuckled and raised our bottles.

"When did you get back?" asked Buzzard.

"Just now. I got out as part of a new early release program the governor started. It's called the Governor's Initiative of Forgiveness and Trust, GIFT for short. Ain't that cute? I'd built up enough time with good behavior and all to make the short list. Plus, I think my aunt over in Indiana pulled some strings or something. As soon as I got out, I hopped on the next bus, grabbed my truck at home, and came right here."

"Why here?"

Lonny cleared his throat with another swig. "If you must know, years ago, right over there by the swimming hole, I nearly lost my life. Do you guys know who Dante Alagori is?"

We all chimed in about knowing Dante, and Lonny continued with his story. "When I was around twelve years old, I saw Dante downtown and started teasing him. He got a good look at me as I ran away and shouted back, 'You're Joseph's boy, aren't you? I'll get you, you little shit.' You can imagine how I felt after that. I'd been made, and he knew right where to find me. Anyway, Dante was drinking up at Hank's one night when he overheard my dad talking about how I was camping out at the dam, trying to earn a Boy Scout badge. That's, of course, before they kicked me out because of another misunderstanding."

A little side note is necessary about Lonny's brief but colorful Boy Scout career: Apparently, he thought they should have a merit badge for scalping. Since he was one-quarter Cherokee, he took it upon himself to create the guidelines. When he submitted the paperwork along with a scalped rabbit as evidence, the council politely asked him to never come back.

Anyway, back to Lonny's story.

"Dante found me later that night over there, across the cove, camping near the swimming hole. He pulled out a knife the size of a machete and was going to cut off both my ears and my bottom lip. You know what happens when you cut off someone's bottom lip, don't ya?" We all shook our heads as he raised his bottle in the air. "You be sipping from a straw for the rest of your life…Imagine that, boys." With that, he chugged the rest of the beer and tossed it into the truck bed.

"So as I was saying, Dante had me in a chokehold and was ready to go Sushi Chef on me when he noticed my tattoo." Lonny held out his left arm, and written in blue on the underside was the name Betty Lou. "Well, come to find out that his dead wife's name was Betty Lou, just like my mom's. That seemed to snap him out of his anger fit, and he let me go. He just stood there for the longest time without saying a word. I was too afraid to move but still crying like a baby, you know, trying to get a hold of myself and all. Finally, I got enough courage up to look at him, and, sure enough, he was crying, too. The next thing you know, we were exchanging stories about our long-lost ladies and had become buddies."

"So why do you keep coming out here?" asked Buzzard.

Lonny rubbed his hands together. "Hell, I don't know. I guess it makes me remember just how lucky I am to still be alive. Plus, sometimes Dante hangs out down by the river and fishes, so I bring him a six pack or two." He gazed over to the riverbank. "I guess he'd be a fool to be fishing tonight, wouldn't he?" The memory of Dante chugging a Pabst Blue Ribbon beer that morning I'd met him now made more sense. Then Lonny looked at each of us. "So what in tarnation are you boys doing out here?"

"We *were* playing hockey," griped Skeeter.

Lonny looked around at the hockey sticks. "So you guys quit already?"

Skeeter waved an arm. "Not by our choice. Old dipshit here shot the puck out on the lake."

"Hey, it was an accident."

"Who cares? The game is over." I added.

"Not necessarily," hummed Lonny. "I hear it's been below zero for a good two weeks now, right?"

"Yeah, but—"

"Yeah, but what?" he interrupted as he walked over to the river's edge and jumped down on the ice. Then he stomped on it a few more times. "Looks solid enough."

"You going to walk out there?" asked T.J.

"Hell no, I'm gonna drive. How else can I see the puck?"

He ran back to the truck, opened the door, and shouted, "Anyone want to come along?"

He took our silence as a no and fired up his old Chevy. Without hesitation, Lonny backed up and drove down to the loading ramp. Then he slowly placed the front tires on the ice and listened. "Here goes nothin'," he yelled as a shot of gray smoke plumed out of the tailpipe. He drove over the snowbank onto the middle of the cove and carefully climbed the other snow bank at the edge. His headlights were lighting up the rest of the lake now, and we heard him shout, "There it is."

The truck shifted into second gear and rolled out onto the middle of the lake as the tires spun on the slick ice. While his beat-up, old pickup spun figure eights and circles around the puck, he let out a holler that echoed for miles downriver. A few minutes later, he opened the door and swooped up the puck, causing us all to cheer.

Then we heard a siren blast so loud that it nearly knocked us into the fire. "Come off the ice immediately," the cop ordered over the loudspeaker as his car slowly made its way up to the cove. When we looked back, Lonny had turned the lights off on his truck and was sitting in the middle of the lake. The cop car shined his spotlight on it as the snow started to fall. The naked trees surrounding the lake were now laced in white but did little to stop the wind from blowing and soon Lonny's truck was a pale image of itself.

"You have sixty seconds," the speaker commanded.

Sixty seconds or what? I thought. I'm pretty sure Officer Hightower had no intention of putting his life in danger and going out on the ice after the truck. What was he going to do when the time was up? He climbed out of the car and shined his flashlight over the lake. All he saw was the silhouette of a man in the driver's seat. The window was down, and the snow was still swirling around the truck like a cotton candy machine. Lonny adjusted his rear view mirror to get a better look but kept his back toward the light. During the brief moments when the air stood still and allowed the swirling snow to take a breather, their eyes met in the reflection of that mirror. This only confirmed what they both already knew.

At this point, it was more an issue of pride than anything to do with law and order. Lonny stared back in defiance, just daring Hightower to come after him. Hightower glared back just waiting for Lonny to make a wrong move. What had started out years ago as a scuffle between a rebel child bending the laws and an officer sworn to uphold them, had grown into a high stakes game of chicken. Unfortunately, both sides were so damn stubborn that neither one would blink.

They faced off for a few minutes until the snow started to really come down. The skies were now glowing white while the moon hid behind layers of clouds. An army of snowflakes silently parachuted to the ground. Lonny revved up the engine and signaled that he was tired of this game by saluting Hightower with a thumbs up. We barely heard his screams over the engine noise as the truck sped away down the river a half a mile to the Lakeview Leisure Club boat dock. The ice shifted and croaked out new surface cracks along the trail following his tire marks. Air bubbles sprung up to the top and recoiled like a Slinky being tossed down the stairs. Lonny still had his lights off, but we caught glimpses of the red glow coming from his breaks as he pulled up onto land.

Then it happened. One of those rare moments when your faith in the Almighty is reaffirmed and you realize that a chapter in a person's life has just been punctuated with a comma instead of a period. As soon as his truck drove up on the concrete ramp down at the Leisure Club, the ice behind him collapsed and sank into the water. There was no mistaking that sound of rushing water flowing on the top, and we all heard it. Hightower rushed back to his car and aimed his spotlight into the distance. A dark blue hole the size of a large yacht was belching up water onto the surface. Lonny's brake lights glistened off the reflection, confirming that he was indeed safe. Then they disappeared up the road.

The Chief just banged his flashlight against his palm and growled, "Someday that boy's gonna push me too far." And with that, he got back in the car, turned on the siren, and tore off in pursuit. Of course, by the time he'd made it around the lake using a loosely connected rectangular grid of country roads, Lonny was long gone.

But Hightower's anger remained.

Chapter Eight

Mrs. Dukas continued to come into the store on a regular basis, complaining about how much money her husband was losing. She was, after all, the trust fund child who'd inherited a fortune from Daddy to live in the nicest house near the lake and run the biggest enterprise in town. Alistair Dukas, on the other hand, had grown up in one of the roughest parts of New York City. His father ran a small bakery, and that's where he honed his business skills both off and on the streets. Fortunately, his charming demeanor, quick wit, and decent looks soon caught the attention of a small-town girl visiting her aunt one summer. The next thing you know, they were married, and Alistair was soon running the family store. No one was quite sure if they married for love or money. Either way, it turned out to be a very convenient arrangement for all parties.

My conversations with Angie, as her parents argued behind walls too thin to hide the animosity between them, went delightfully well. She could transform a cobweb-laden ceiling into a multicolored nebula just by waving her hands upward as she told stories about her travels. The dusty sales floor seemed to glow under her feet as she pranced around, looking at the merchandise. She'd bring a soda pop or candy bar to share while we passed the time. I found her to be extraordinarily bright. It was obvious that the private tutoring and piano lessons had lifted her to a level of sophistication usually only found in larger cities. She talked about theater and ballet as if she'd just attended every premier on Broadway and the Metropolitan Opera House. She entertained me for hours.

Lonny started working in his dad's shop on a daily basis that year, too. Part of the early release agreement with the State meant that he had to remain fully employed while being on probation. Lonny soon realized that no one else was going to hire him just for liability reasons alone. Besides, he had a real talent for finding and selling used items just like his father. He had perfected the art of dumpster diving in the middle of the night. With a flashlight in one hand and a keen eye for spotting discarded treasures, he scoured the alleys of Kickapoo County once a week the night before trash pickup. It couldn't have come at a better time as Joseph Nack was nearing retirement age and walking a little slower every day.

When word surfaced that the Legendary Lonny Nack was working at the shop, in the flesh, business doubled. People came from miles around just for the opportunity to meet the man and maybe, if the mood was right, strike up a conversation about one of his adventures. Lonny was more than happy to oblige. He loved the notoriety and relished every moment of being the main attraction. The stories grew in size just like the store's profit margin.

Most customers didn't even notice the subtle embellishments here and there. Lonny was never at a loss for words and could yarn together two or three completely separate events into one epic adventure, given enough time. He could talk about a grain elevator as if it was a New York skyscraper. He could saw through time frames and hammer together events in a way that made you think he, alone, was responsible for them happening. And the way his eyes lit up between tales of car chases and a lover's loss...Well, let's just say that he never left you feeling disappointed.

No one was prouder and happier about Lonny's progress than Sally. She'd done her best to help out around the shop, but her age and no bullshit style left her feeling uncomfortable around customers. Now that Lonny was there, she took over the domestic duties and made sure everything else ran smoothly. When her father asked her to take over the books, she didn't hesitate to dive in. Joseph finally had his prayers answered. A clear path to succession was in place and retirement was close at hand.

Lonny cornered me one day, many months later after getting out of prison to discuss another subject. I was finishing up lunch at the diner and was ready to leave when he walked in and sat down. He came right out and asked what my future plans were with his sister, given our relationship was so off and on. It was somewhat cute, you know, the way he insinuated that if I ever made her cry he'd break every bone in my body.

But then he changed his tone completely and said, "Newbie, how's the harmonica playing going?"

"Pretty good. Buzzard let me borrow his Paul Butterfield Blues Band album and gave me an old harmonica his dad had in the key of E."

"We should get together and jam sometime."

"Cool."

He put his legs up on the seat and took a sip of my soda. Then he said, "You know what it's like to lose a mother, so I guess you can kind of relate to what I'm about to tell you. When we lost Mama, Sally was only seven years old. She didn't understand what was going on. In fact, she still doesn't know to this day what really happened."

Lonny seemed a little fidgety as he stirred my drink with the straw. There was an unnatural twitch in his shoulder. "We told her it was a heart attack, but the truth is…she killed herself."

"Wow, I didn't know."

"Yeah, no one knows." He scooted up in the seat, looked me in the eye, and continued, "You see, she had this rare disease. It's called Huntington's Chorea, and it messes with your brain and all kinds of other things in your body. Sally had no idea what was happening that day. I'd been told to take her over to the park across from the hospital and play with her on the swings for a while. When Pop finally came back and told us that Mama had died, well…I was just devastated. I'd have never known the truth if it wasn't for overhearing the nurses talking about a suicide victim on their floor. When they carted her out on the gurney, it was pretty easy to tell that they were talking about my mama."

He scratched the back of his head and finished my soda. Then he swallowed hard before saying, "The worst part about it is that it's hereditary. Someday, maybe fifty years from now, maybe tomorrow, either one of us could start slurring our speech, hallucinating, or become so depressed that we don't want to live anymore. According to what I read in a journal over at the library, there's a 50/50 chance that Sally will get it eventually, but we don't know yet. And right now, we don't want her to know."

The long silence that followed in that booth wasn't uneasy. In fact, it wasn't even awkward. It was more introspective than anything. I say that with the best intentions as no one would ever wish that kind of illness on anyone else, but, at that moment, I sensed that Lonny was telling me this revelation more for his own sake than for Sally's.

He inhaled and slowly let it out. Then he reflected, "You know, Newbie, life is a paradox. We hope that tomorrow will bring a better day, but, in reality, it just brings us one day closer to death. Kind of absurd, isn't it?" He unrolled a cigarette pack from his shirtsleeve and tapped on the end of it. "You read much?"

"Yeah, well, you know. We have to read all kinds of things in English class, but I read some other stuff on the side."

"If you ever get a chance, pick up one of Albert Camus's books. It'll change your life."

"For better or worse?"

He chuckled. "Touché. Yeah, you're right. Most of his stuff was pretty depressing, but he did have some interesting perspectives on life and death."

A mist began to fall outside, and Lonny seemed to be mesmerized by the whole scene. Tiny water droplets blanketed the window, creating a picturesque view right out of a Monet painting. Not knowing where this conversation was going, I got a little nervous and said the first thing that came to mind. "So what you're saying is that you should live your life to the fullest. What did you say a while back, 'No blood, no foul?'"

Lonny shook his head. "No, not like that. I guess what I'm trying to say is—she's all I got. She's all I remember about Mama. Sally has the same eyes, the same nose, and the same giggle. And in the right light, usually about suppertime, I'll see her messing around in the kitchen, humming a little out of tune, just like Mama…And in that moment, she *is* Mama…So, if I ever lose Sally, I lose them both, forever."

Lonny turned away before I could see his eyes water. Then he grabbed his keys and said, "You ever heard of the Code of Chivalry?"

"No."

"It's about mutual respect, a secret code between men to be upheld at any cost, even death. In other words, keep your mouth shut about what I just said, and if you ever decide to get serious with my sister, you now know the risks…so you'd better be ready to take care of her." He pulled a cigarette out of his pack and placed it in his mouth. "Later."

And with that, he was gone.

By the end of the school year, we'd almost perfected the craft of playing practical jokes and were constantly trying to outdo each other with bigger and better pranks. Buzzard and I loved bringing cars to a skidding halt with the fake rope trick but that got old quickly. T.J. could switch out a speed limit sign with a stop sign in a matter of seconds. After a while though, people quit stopping altogether so we put a moratorium on that one. Switching realtor signs from one house to another was always worth a good laugh. Skeeter had made it a point of sticking as many For Sale signs as he could in the front yard of any teacher who gave him a bad grade. Of course, none of these deeds compared to Lonny's list of accomplishments. We were still learning the art of raising hell and were not quite ready to move up to his league.

Revenge may not be a heavenly virtue, but when served up cold, it is tastier than any flavor of ice cream coming out of the Hum Dinger's tap. Unfortunately, for Billy Hightower, it was served up hot and cold. The Hum Dinger had a chicken sandwich and banana split combo that was so delicious people drove from miles around just to savor a taste. Betsy and Barbara Dinger had run the small business for decades. They were the cutest set of twins you'd ever laid eyes upon, and men would line up around the block just to watch them frolic around inside, dancing to the radio from the cash register to the ice cream tap to the grill and back. When Barbara died unexpectedly of pneumonia, Betsy continued to run the shop on her own in loving memory and dedication to the dream they'd made into reality. Unfortunately, Betsy Dinger didn't quite have the business savvy that her sister, Barbara, had.

Math was never her specialty, so when it came to ordering enough chickens and bananas to last her through the week, she never did quite get it right. More often than not during the high volume season from May to August, she'd make the trip down to the Grab-It-Here, flirt with the store manager for a few minutes, and talk him into discounting a few groceries to last her until the next shipment arrived. Sometimes she'd return to work so giddy from her little fling that she'd completely forget why she'd left in the first place. The food would sit in the car until one of the employees asked her about it later. She'd run out and retrieve it just before the aroma had a chance to seep into her cloth upholstery.

We were minding our own business one day, nibbling on chicken sandwiches and ice cream while watching the cars drive up and down Main Street. It was Saturday afternoon, and every teenager around was cruising the streets looking for some action. You quickly learned to recognize everybody's car by the second or third pass through town. There were teenage girls crammed into their mother's station wagon, singing songs and waving out the window, football players standing in the back of a pickup truck yelling, "We're number one," and a few nerds trying their best to look cool in their daddy's Cadillac. Although I hate to admit it, I knew more about the kind of car some people drove as opposed to the kind of person they were. It was life in rural America where one stoplight, two gas stations, and three different ways to order ice cream meant everything was good in the world.

Like I said, we were just sitting there, without a care in the world, in Skeeter's beat-up convertible Triumph, with its scuffed up British Racing Green paint job and faded brown interior, waving to the talent driving by, when Billy Hightower pulled in. His daddy had just bought him a brand new red Pontiac Trans Am 455 with a V8 engine, pumping out 300 horsepower with 415 pounds of torque. It was the sexiest badass machine on the road, and we hated him for it. He and his monkey posse pulled into the Hum Dinger and started teasing Skeeter about his car before they'd even turned off the engine.

"How's the Skeeter beater running today?"

"Go eff yourself, Billy."

"Hey now, that's no way to be talking. I was just asking since I haven't seen it around for a while. What do you call it? Pickles or Cucumber or something?"

"It's been in the garage, and just for the record, I get more pussy with that car sitting in my garage than you get with yours on the street, waving hundred dollar bills out the window."

We spilled over laughing at Skeeter's comment. Billy and his band of bums closed in and surrounded the car. "I don't know if I'd call banging Sally Nack, 'Getting pussy,' considering she probably gave you a couple of gifts to remember her by. You might want to call it 'Getting VD,' instead." Then he turned to me. "You probably know about that too, Johnson, considering you've been fingering her since she was twelve."

I was out of the front seat with my fists clenched and ready to do battle when T.J. grabbed my shoulder. "I got this, dude."

"No, I got this one." He could see the anger boiling over inside me.

"No, he's baiting you, man. Not here. Not now. Let me take the first crack." Then he winked at me.

I took a deep breath and nodded. T.J. smoothly slid out of the back seat over the side panel, and stood before Billy, towering four inches above him. "If it wasn't for your daddy, you'd be dead right now." Then he placed the tip of his sneakers on Billy's toes and crushed them like a cigarette butt while adding, "I think you owe us an apology for that comment."

Billy backed up a step, did his best to hold in his gut, and scrunched up his bleached out eyebrows. Then he snorted, "In your dreams. Go ask my dad for an apology." The two stared each other down for what seemed like an eternity. We were all ready to jump into action, but as time dragged on, Billy had to exhale, releasing a molten layer of stomach that completely covered his belt and hips. T.J., on the other hand, had been conditioning for football every morning. His tight abs and muscles were bulging out of his T-shirt as he took the last bite of his sandwich. I don't know if the two digestive systems connected on a telepathic level or not, but Billy's stomach immediately started growling, so he turned to the others and said, "Let's get some lunch." T.J. and Buzzard had to hold Skeeter and me down as they walked away. We were fuming.

"I'm going to kill that punk," shot off Skeeter.

You're gonna have to get in line," I retorted.

Buzzard held on tightly and said, "Gentlemen, gentlemen, calm down. You're not thinking straight here. And with that look in your eyes, Newbie, I'm afraid of what you might do once you got a hold of him."

"I don't care. I'm not going to let him get away with spouting off like that."

"We're on the same page, my friend, the same page. I'm just reading between the lines and you're not."

"What do you mean?"

His eyes narrowed and focused on Billy and his gang off in the distance. He had the determination of Dirty Harry with the mindset of Dr. Jekyll. It was dangerous, yet exuberating. He exhaled and added, "I mean that throughout mankind, humans have tussled with the irresistible urge to act instinctively in these situations, thus, usually leaving oneself in a compromising position. Are we to lose all sense of dignity when seeking out our revenge and rush into judgment, or should we tread lightly and thoughtfully? We must remember that the most expedient method is not always the most satisfying."

Skeeter gazed into Buzzard's eyes for the longest time. He didn't flinch, he didn't blink, and he didn't even breathe. I could only assume that he was still digesting Buzzard's comments and trying to make sense of them all. After a while, he sighed. "Sometimes you scare the living shit out of me. Where in the hell did you learn to talk like that?"

You could tell that Skeeter's words embarrassed Buzzard a bit by the way he lowered his head and replied, "I don't know. What do you want me to say? I guess I just read a lot."

Skeeter smiled. "It's okay, Stud. I love every word that comes out of your mouth. Can you just translate them into regular English so the rest of us understand?"

"Sure. What I'm trying to say here is that we don't get mad; we get even. What do you think is going to happen as soon as you beat the crap out of Billy, huh? His dad is going to stop us every time we drive down Main Street. No, we have to be as sly as a fox, here."

"And do what?" I asked.

Buzzard floated a grin the size of Mount Rushmore that day, which I'll remember for as long as I live. He didn't say another word as he grabbed an empty mason jar out of the dumpster behind the Hum Dinger, slipped into Ms. Dinger's back seat and squeezed a pound of uncooked chicken inside the jar. Then he sprinkled the rest of his ice cream over the top, tightened the cap as hard as he could, and wedged the jar under Billy's front car seat.

Now maybe you aren't familiar with the chemical reaction between rotting chicken and curdling milk byproducts, but I can guarantee you that Buzzard was. We didn't even have to ask what would eventually happen to that jar after boiling in the hot sun for a week or two. We already knew. When it finally exploded that sweltering day as the Butt Crack Gang was cruising through town, spilling onto their shoes, ruining the carpet and splattering inside the seat cushion, we felt vindicated.

Chapter Nine

By our junior year, Buzzard was escorting us around in a Dodge Charger, every gas station in town had a sign that said, "Pay Before You Pump," and I was in a full-blown relationship with Angie Dukas. Although I would always have a place in my heart for Sally, we just never seemed to be able to get on the same page when it came to romance. She had way too much going on at home to bother with silly little things like boyfriends. Angie, on the other hand, had all the time in the world. She had this indescribable quality and mystery surrounding her that always made me want to know more. Her delivery was polished in every way, she didn't have a penchant for fighting, and she could care less about normal everyday tasks like watering the plants, cleaning her room, and washing her own clothes. She emitted affluence from her pores like it was some exotic perfume.

Another plus was that her father surrendered the keys to his convertible Mustang any time she asked. We'd take off and grab an ice cream cone at the Hum Dinger, catch the latest movie at the drive-in, or just cruise the countryside until we got lost. We were knee deep in cornfields and soybeans for as far as the eye could see. The small villages dotting the back roads of Kickapoo County were our playgrounds, and we enjoyed every minute of it. Cornfields zipped by like spokes on a bicycle wheel as we ventured over to the abandoned coal mines. On top of the man-made pyramids of shale and fossils, carbon bubbled up from underneath the surface, warming our bodies as we watched a kaleidoscope of clouds paint the landscape over the flat, open prairie.

Eventually, we would end up back at the dam and Bunsen Lake. Parked next to the waterfall, we'd watch the fishermen cast their lines from the banks and boats. The robins and cardinals paraded back and forth from trees to picnic tables, dining on leftovers and showing off their plumage. Row after row of maple, oak, and birch trees cushioned the shorelines. The different shades of green blended in so well with the lighter blues bubbling up from the roaring water. It wasn't postcard perfect, but it was as close to heaven as you could get in Bunsen Creek.

I'd bet that more babies were created on that spot than any other place in town. I found myself mesmerized by the moment so passionately that I was ready to open up and confess everything. Even those three romantic words the boys and I swore never to speak in the presence of the opposite sex. As I stared into her warm, brown eyes, my hand trembling on the gearshift, I fumbled for the right way to begin my declaration when…"Do you want to go see a movie?" plopped out of my mouth.

Angie just smiled. She knew she had me under her spell. The expression on my face said it all. She turned the key and replied, "Sure."

There was a two-for-one matinee playing that afternoon. I don't remember the name of the first film now, but I do remember seeing Vincent Price laughing with bloodstained hands. The second was *The Godfather*. The gang and I had seen it a hundred times by now, but it never got old. Apparently, something about gangsters brought out the nasty side of Angie as I spent most of the movie inside her mouth. Buzzard and T.J. were sitting on the other side of the theater in the last row with the Foster sisters, buried knee deep in their own erotic sideshow. Every once in a while, I'd hear giggling coming from their section or get a thumbs-up when we made eye contact.

The theater was more than half full. Old Man Tranchant did a good job of keeping the place profitable with discounted matinees and cheap popcorn. Even though he owned half of the valley southeast of town, the man was a miser when it came to spending money. He would never pay for new features on their first release but instead recycled them months later with other films. He'd package together two of the best pictures of the year and offered them for the price of one. I use the word "recycled" because that was his favorite word. He was the first environmentalist to practice recycling and land conservation in Kickapoo County. Between catching his own rainwater, composting fallen leaves, and making sure the wildlife around Bunsen Creek remained unharmed, you couldn't find another person more dedicated to saving the planet.

About halfway through the second feature, I smelled smoke. Then Angie turned to me and said, "Do you smell something?"

Sure enough, other people started grumbling, and, before long, a few of them were getting out of their seats to investigate. "Let's head out the back door and see what's going on."

When I opened the door to the alley, a plume of grey smoke swooped around from the building next to us and stung my eyes. "Holy crap!" I gasped as I pushed Angie and myself outside.

A fire had completely engulfed the east side of the hardware store on the corner of the block. It had spread into the bottom floor of the apartment building, which was connected to the theater. The only other person in the alley besides us was Colonel Remus P. Entwhistle, who was waving his white Bible and screaming scripture at the flames like he was scolding an unruly child. T.J. and Buzzard soon appeared with their dates and rushed over to where we were standing.

"How the heck did this happen?" asked Buzzard.

"Looks like it started in the hardware store."

About that time, Lonny came barreling out of the backdoor of the apartment building in between the hardware store and theater, carrying a young girl. She was coughing and scared but looked to be unscathed by the flames. "There might be more on the second floor. Newbie, give me a hand," he shouted.

The Colonel was now standing at the doorway, shuffling moviegoers out of the theater and yelling, "Get as far away as you can. The whole second floor is filled with old film canisters."

"Old film canisters," repeated T.J.

"Yeah, sometimes the cellulous nitrate becomes unstable."

"Cellulous nitrate?"

"Nitroglycerin you idiots," shouted the Colonel. "Get out of here!"

Lonny brushed off the young girl and handed her to Angie. "I'm going back in there. There's an old lady living on the top floor that used to come into our shop. She's been sick lately, and I know she's still in there."

"We're going with you," said T.J.

And with that, the three of us followed Lonny up the stairs to the second and third floors looking for stragglers. "Kick in the doors and check every apartment," shouted Lonny.

We could hear the Colonel scolding us from below, "You'd better get out of there and let the fire department handle this." Of course, his comment was almost as comical as it was misguided. The emergency siren hadn't even gone off yet, so the volunteers down at the station were never going to make it in time.

A cloud of smoke had quickly filled up the second floor, but there weren't any flames yet. Lonny screamed, "Anybody in there?" Seconds later, he kicked in another door and ran in. The three of us followed and scoped out each room shouting and searching for victims. After clearing the second story, we raced up to the third floor. Someone was calling from inside the apartment on the north end.

"Mrs. Blanche, is that you?" shouted Lonny.

"Yes," came a muffled cry from the other side of the door.

"Stand back," he said as he shredded the wooden jamb with one kick. We all rushed in and rifled through the rooms while yelling her name. "Mrs. Blanche, where are you?"

"Back here."

When we followed the sound into the bedroom, the three of us stopped dead in our tracks. Sitting on the bed, stuffed into a nightgown that more closely resembled a curtain was Mrs. Blanche—all three hundred pounds of her.

"Oh my god," I moaned as Lonny ran to her side.

"Can you walk?" he asked.

"No, my feet are swollen…gout."

The four of us locked eyes for a moment and didn't say a word. Part of me just wanted to run down the stairs and wait for the fire department. The better part of me knew that wasn't an option.

"What are we gonna do?" I asked.

Lonny scanned the room like a lighthouse looking for a sinking ship. His eyes pinged from one item to another as the heat rose from our feet.

"The chair. Let's carry her down," said Buzzard.

Lonny nodded. "Why not? Good idea, whoever the hell you are."

"That's Buzzard and this is T.J. You met them at the dam when we were ice skating."

Lonny grinned. "Oh yeah. You and those damn nicknames."

I grabbed the chair and placed it next to the bed. Then Mrs. Blanche scooted over to the edge and said, "Help me, boys."

There was no way that all four of us could get a grip on her so Lonny and T.J. did the honors. Mind you, lifting three hundred pounds of flab was like trying to pick up a thirty-three gallon bag full of water. She slid from one set of fingers to the other while they wrestled with handfuls of blubber and reached into crevices that hadn't been touched in decades. Finally, they were able to waddle her into the chair.

"Okay, everyone grab a corner."

"No, wait. Where's Tiny?" screamed Mrs. Blanche.

"Tiny?"

"My cat."

Lonny rubbed his head and spun around in a circle. I could tell he just wanted to explode and say something about the flames and smoke sifting up through the register being more important. Instead, he took a deep breath and counted to ten under his breath.

"Under the bed. I saw her run under there," said Buzzard.

I peered under the bed, and there was no cat. Then I hopped over to the other side and there she was: Tiny. A twenty-five pound brown, black and white Maine Coon with eyes the color of silver dollars and a set of lobster sized sharp claws. I didn't even hesitate as I reached in, grabbed her by the fur, and yanked the king-size feline out from under the bed. I did everything possible to keep from letting go as the cat tattooed my arm with scratches. The other guys ducked out of the way as the tail and back paws kicked and screamed in the air. Then, as soon as it felt Mrs. Blanche's reassuring lap, it immediately started purring.

"Alright, problem solved. Good job, Newbie. Everyone grab a leg and let's get out of here."

Navigating the doorway was hard enough considering that the chair and body were rubbing against the walls. Two of us had to grab the bottom of the chair instead of the legs in order to move it forward. When we came to the staircase, a wall of smoke was waiting for us.

"I can't breathe," cried T.J.

"Grab some clothes from her drawer and wrap them around your nose," replied Lonny.

We set the chair down while T.J. and Buzzard went back to the bedroom searching for something to wear. They came back with a couple of slips and a blouse that smelled like body odor dipped in soured milk.

I put my elbow up to my nose. "You've got to be kidding. That's all there is?"

Lonny tore the slip in half and handed a garment to each of us. "It's better than nothing, boys. Grin and bear it."

A thick cloud of smoke was now hovering at the top of the stairs. The only thing we saw on the landing down on the second floor was a growing number of flames trickling out around the side doors. We didn't have much time.

"Jesus, Newbie, what do we do?" whispered T.J. "Getting this chair down those stairs before the flames get us is gonna be…"

"…Gonna be alright, if we stick together." I grabbed both their arms and asked, "We're family, right?"

They both immediately nodded.

"What's Mama Corleone say to Michael? 'You always have your family, right?' We do this together." The boys didn't seem to mind that I'd botched the whole quote from the movie we'd just seen. The important factor was that they got the underlining message.

"Let's do this," replied T.J. as we all three shook hands.

I didn't really have time to analyze the meaning of this moment, as I was more worried about getting out of that building alive. It wasn't until later on did I realize that we had grown that close over the years. They were the brothers I'd never had, and Skeeter's mom and dad were the surrogate parents I'd always wished for. That day, it was more about instinct as opposed to insight though.

Lonny had been busy tying Mrs. Blanche into the chair with her bath robe belt while the three of us talked among ourselves. When she was secure and tight, he moved to the front and said, "Alright everyone, grab a leg and work together one step at a time. No one let go, 'cause if you do, we all go down. Understood?"

We paused after each step and made eye contact. When all four of us moved as one, the chair didn't seem that heavy. Stair after stair, we descended with no problems. About halfway down near the next landing, one of the doors on the second level collapsed and a deluge of flames rushed up the steps. T.J. lost his grip and footing when the fire briefly scorched his back. "Damn that's hot." The chair slipped out of his hands, and he sunk to his knees.

Lonny moved to the center and yelled, "Focus boys. I'm losing her." The chair tilted sideways while the full weight of her body collapsed into Lonny's arms, sending him sliding down two more steps. "T.J., I need you," he screamed. It was the only time in my life that I'd ever seen fear in the man's eyes. He stooped down on his knees and braced for the worse as his shoes slid out from under him. It was just his brute strength against nature. Buzzard and I pushed against the walls and tried to hold on but the momentum had shifted out of our favor.

"We're losing her."

As the fire licked the staircase walls, I realized at that moment what being human really meant. Sure, having feelings and a conscience set us apart from the rest of the animal kingdom, but being human also means being vulnerable and mortal. No matter how we tried to ignore that simple fact, it always caught up with us in the end. Lonny shouted again, but the words were muffled as the crackling heat bellowed and pounded its combustible chest from below. We were losing Lonny and T.J. fast.

That's when a small miracle happened. As Lonny and T.J. struggled to hold on, Mrs. Blanche reached up and latched onto the railing. She may have been three hundred pounds of flab on the outside, but inside, the woman had the grip of a sailor's square knot.

The chair stabilized just long enough for both of them to secure the legs. Buzzard and I repositioned our holds and let out a sigh of relief. Mrs. Blanche had one hand clamped on Tiny's nape and the other firmly strangling the banister.

"Let's do this."

Not another word was said as we shuffled from one step to the other as fast as we could and carted the chair out the back door. All of us walked blindly down the last few steps because the blackened smoke had rendered our eyesight useless. Only when the sunlight broke through in the alley were we able to exhale. We carried Mrs. Blanche to the end of the block where Fat Ferny and Hightower were waiting next to an ambulance. Everybody else had been evacuated and sanctioned to watching from three blocks away due to the unknown dangers lurking in the theater storeroom.

As they loaded Mrs. Blanche into the ambulance, Lonny said, "Boys, thank you for helping. I couldn't have done it without you."

"No problem, Lonny. You'd done the same thing for us." I added.

"You're right, my friends. I would've, and from now on, you can just count on it."

"I hope she'll be alright," remarked Buzzard.

"Oh, she'll be fine." Lonny smiled and put his hand on my shoulder. Then he said, "We're all gonna be fine, aren't we?"

I wasn't quite sure what he meant by that last statement. With all of the confusion and excitement, it just rolled off his tongue and out of my mind. It wasn't until much later did those words take on a life of their own. But, I'll leave it at that, for now.

"Everyone, move across the street. Smoke is coming out of the top of the theater," shouted Hightower.

We stood and watched another half hour as the firemen doused the remaining flames and reduced them to a smolder with tints of blue and black swirling into the evening sky. The reporters were there, blending in with the rest of the town that gathered along the perimeter. Traffic had been averted blocks away and the square looked like a ghost town. All of a sudden, the roof of the theater blasted apart like a volcano, shooting a cannon fire progression of cinders and embers into the atmosphere. The flames died down quickly but film canisters continued to explode every few minutes. We waited like children lying on the hillside at the Lakeview Leisure Club anticipating the next round of fireworks. Canisters rocketed onto the streets and slowly rose from the ground into curling columns of ash as the celluloid burned away. From a distance, they resembled black snake fireworks sizzling up off the sidewalks and slithering back down to their final resting place.

We all recounted our stories to the police and newspapers during the next few hours while the firemen finished their jobs. Then we went home for the night, mentally and physically exhausted. Angie and the others had left hours before since no one was allowed inside the perimeter but essential personnel. It wasn't until the next morning that they reopened Main Street for traffic. Buck's Diner had escaped the wrath of the fire due to the gallant work of the firemen and a ten-foot alley between the buildings.

The morning newspaper had an aerial view of the square on the front page, showing a quarter of it lying in soot and rubble along with several shots of flames and smoke pouring out of the buildings. "Bunsen Creek Suffers a Black Eye," was the headline. The townsfolk did not overlook the symbolic meaning of the quote. In the back of their minds, they wondered who would ever rebuild the buildings. Plans for a new mall in Carbonville were in the works, touting four well-known hub stores and a multi-theater complex. Who could compete with that?

The insurance companies were already fighting about who was to blame and what caused the fire. Old Man Tranchant, who owned three quarters of the block from the hardware store to the theater, had been found dead in the rubble the next morning. His charred body was identified only after dental records were retrieved. He obviously didn't burn the buildings down to collect the insurance money, but there were traces of gasoline in places they shouldn't have been. Of course, it was a hardware store so having gallons of gasoline in the back room wasn't unusual, considering that he also worked on broken lawn mowers.

The old man didn't have any relatives so that meant there would be lawyers and adjusters jousting over decimal points and payouts for years to come. Even if there was a settlement, the chances of it going back into the community to rebuild were slim. It was apparent that a big part of the breathing apparatus keeping our downtown alive had been surgically removed. Our community was now on life support, and with that, a part of our childhood slowly disappeared from memory. As time went by, talk of rebuilding was swept up and carted away with the rubble. People were more excited with the new mall in Carbonville and eventually became complacent with the new look of the square. Or should I say, the lack of it.

Chapter Ten

News of our heroics spread throughout the town quickly, and we couldn't go anywhere without someone patting us on the back and making us regret we'd ever set foot in that movie theater. The praise for Lonny went from admiration to suspicion overnight after the police finally caught up to Colonel Entwhistle and interviewed him. They had their doubts about Entwhistle's story considering that he'd left the scene of the crime before being questioned and spent the rest of the night at Hank's Oasis. They may have overlooked him altogether if it weren't for Angie pointing out in her debriefing that he'd been there in the alley. Yet, just having a slight possibility of pinning the fire on Lonny was worth investigating.

Lonny was back at work the next day in his dad's store when Hightower and Ferny walked in. Sally was manning the cash register while her father was out back helping a customer load their truck. It didn't take long after the policeman greeted the two siblings before they started interrogating Lonny. One thing led to another and before you knew it, they had Lonny handcuffed and in the back seat of the cop car. They cited a violation of probation after smelling whiskey on his breath as the excuse.

Sally called me shortly after the cops carted Lonny off to jail. I was hesitant to answer since most calls that morning were coming from reporters and neighbors asking questions, but something told me to pick up this time.

"Newbie, it's Sally. They've taken Lonny down to the jail again." She was sobbing between breaths.

"What for?"

"They think he started the fire. They said something about Colonel Entwhistle smelling gasoline on Lonny's clothes as he passed him in the alley."

"The Colonel. And they believed him?"

"Guess so."

"If he had gas on his clothes, then he would've gone up in flames when we pulled Mrs. Blanche out of the building."

"That's true. Can you meet me down at the station?"

"I'm on my way."

I called Skeeter and filled him in on the story. He lived just a block away from city hall, so I asked him to meet me there. Then I hopped on my Kawasaki and tore down the street, running every stop sign along the way. There are advantages and disadvantages to having only one cop car in town. If there ever was a real emergency, waiting on back-up could be the difference between life and death. On the other hand, when you knew that the police were in one particular spot, that meant the whole town was yours to plunder and pillage. I was at city hall in less than two minutes.

City hall was a square building smaller than most houses in the neighborhood. There was a larger room used for meetings as you walked in off the streets. Over to the side was a room with a few desks for the mayor and his secretary, and, in the rear, were two jail cells and the sheriff's office. The sheriff's office doubled as the interrogation room, reception's desk, and command center, fully equipped with a scanner, radio, and copy machine. On the wall, to the right of the American flag was a picture frame containing Chief Hightower's Korean War Service Medal. Next to that was a photo of a much younger Hightower dressed in uniform standing next to President Harry Truman. I arrived just as they were about to write up the paperwork.

Out of breath and pumped up on adrenaline, I asked, "What's going on here?"

Hightower took one look at me and replied, "Son, this has nothing to do with you so I suggest that—"

"If it has to do with the fire, then it has something to do with me, and I think I deserve an explanation."

He set down his pen and looked over to Fat Ferny. Then, in a cadence that only a staff sergeant could deliver, he yelled, "Get the hell out of here before I throw your ass in the cell."

I stood there, stunned, trapped inside a body that neither moved nor understood. His words had plucked the feathers right out of my emotional war bonnet and left me speechless.

"And if we don't," came Skeeter's voice from behind. He placed his hand on my shoulder, winked, and whispered, "How you doing, Stud?"

Chief Hightower closed his eyes, hung his head down, and swung it back and forth a few times. "Boys, you are interfering with official police business, and I'm not going to tell you again to leave."

"Don't give me any of that official police business bullshit, Tony. I know my rights and you and your little sidekick here don't scare me."

No, he didn't, I said to myself. *Did he just call the chief of police by his first name?* Sometimes Skeeter showed more balls than the Christmas tree at Rockefeller Center.

"Go on guys. I'll be fine," said Lonny who was sitting in a chair next to the desk, sporting a new black eye.

A deep voice, straight out of the Ozarks, said, "Ain't nobody going nowhere." We all turned to see Joseph Nack standing in the doorway with Sally. He walked up, put his hand on his boy, and asked, "How they treating you, son?"

"Like a baby treats a diaper, Pop."

Until that day, I'd never witnessed such an overt display of telepathic influence over one person by another. The old adage, "Stare a hole right through you," came to mind but didn't even come close to describing the way in which Joseph's piercing glare melted Hightower's psyche into the emotional consistency of fondue. There was a brief moment when both sets of eyes stood their ground, and it appeared that the situation could escalate. Hightower did his best to put on a fearless front, but in the end, he realized that defending one's dignity was no match against the powers of unconditional love and family pride.

When the chief succumbed and finally surrendered by turning away, Joseph motioned to Sally, who was holding a paper sack and said, "Go on. Show 'em."

Sally walked over to the desk and opened the bag. Then she pulled out a pair of filthy charcoaled jeans and a dusty pair of tennis shoes. "Here are the clothes Lonny had on yesterday."

Hightower lifted up the jeans with his pen, trying to avoid getting any of the soot on his hands, and took a whiff. Then he knelt down and sniffed the shoes. "Where's the shirt?"

"I didn't have one on," answered Lonny. "Hell, I never wear a shirt in the summer, unless I'm working in the store."

The Chief glanced over at Ferny and said, "Get the Colonel down here right now, and let's settle this once and for all."

Ferny went into the front room and made a phone call. Then he came back in and said, "I'll have to go pick him up. Seems that he doesn't have a driver's license."

"Oh my God," moaned Hightower. "Well, hurry up."

Fat Ferny left out the side door, turned on the red lights, and sped away. Sally hugged her brother for the longest time and whispered something into his ear. Joseph walked up, squeezed his hand, and nodded. The Chief tried to look busy at his desk with paperwork while the rest of us stood there, silent. It was awkward in every sense of the word.

Sally came over a few minutes later and hugged the both of us. "Thank you for coming."

"We got your back, remember," replied Skeeter.

That moment confirmed what I already knew from the day before. The four of us had forged an understanding years before that nothing, and nobody, would ever come between us. We'd proven unequivocally that when faced with danger or hardship, we were going to be there for each other. I wanted to hug Skeeter myself but knew better considering the company we were with.

A few minutes later, the police car pulled up. Fat Ferny led the Colonel through the door and sat him down on the other side of the chief's desk. He glared over at us through his Coke bottle glasses as he waddled by. Everyone in town knew that he wasn't a real colonel. He'd managed to avoid the army draft due to his poor eyesight and picked up the self-bequeathed title one summer while working for his uncle auctioneering. He was maybe a dozen years older than

Lonny, although no one knew for sure. His confident demeanor, balding head and bulging waistline made him look way older than he really was.

No one questioned the man's verbal skills though. In fact, most people avoided conversations with him altogether. You would find the Colonel standing on the corner of Happy and Go Lucky almost any day of the week just waiting for someone to walk by and say "Hello." That single word trapped you into a thirty-minute tirade covering everything from the politics behind the Vietnam War to the apocalyptic arrival of the end of the world.

"Officer, what's this all about?" He was visibly shaken and nervously tapping his fingers on his Bible.

"Well, Colonel, it seems that we have a few inconsistencies with the account you gave us about the fire." Hightower opened his notebook. "Let me look at my notes here. Yeah, here we go. Interview with Remus Entwater…"

"That's Remus P. Entwhistle, Sergeant. You can call me 'Re-Pent' for short," he added as he turned around and winked at us.

"That would be 'Chief' to you, not 'Sergeant.'"

"My apologies, kind sir. Please proceed."

"It says here in my notes that you stated that at approximately 5:30 in the evening, you had just walked through the parking lot of the hardware store. There you saw smoke coming out of the back door and flagged down Alistair Dukas, who was driving by. You asked him to drive over to the fire station and report the incident. Then as you were walking down the alley, you passed by the suspect, Lonny Nack, heading north while you were heading south. Is that correct?"

"It is, sir."

"It also says that when the suspect walked past you, you smelled gasoline. Is that also correct?"

"It is."

"Then you asked the suspect to help you look for people trapped in the buildings."

Lonny had had about as much gospel truth as he could stomach and roared, "That's a bunch of malarkey. I was in the dumpster digging through the trash when you ran by and yelled 'Fire.' I told you to get your ass back there and help me."

"Now, Lonny, you'll get your turn to speak," said Hightower, who looked over at Ferny. "Settle down." Ferny slowly crept in a few steps closer until Lonny whipped around and gave him a piercing glare. He quickly reversed course and backed away.

The Colonel pulled out a white handkerchief and wiped his forehead. Then he returned it to the front pocket on his seersucker suit and replied, "I told you what I saw and nothing more. I'm not the kind of man to bear false witness against another man or disavow any of the Ten Commandments."

"Understood, Colonel, but here are the clothes Lonny was wearing yesterday, and there is no smell of gasoline anywhere on them."

"Well, I don't, I mean, I don't really know what to tell you. I smelled what I smelled."

"Could you be mistaken? After all, those are pretty serious accusations to be making."

He lifted his Bible in the air. "I swear on this Bible that I smelled gasoline as I passed by this man."

Lonny pounded his handcuffed hands on the desk and said, "Chief, this pansy ass nark is just full of horse manure. He's been sore at me ever since I borrowed his hat."

"Borrowed would insinuate that you gave it back, and asked in the first place."

"I asked."

"Telling is not asking."

"Well, I can't give it back."

"And why's that?"

"Because I lost it in a..." The last few words trailed off in an almost muted mumble.

"What was that? I didn't hear you."

"I said I lost it in a poker game."

"Okay, that's enough. I think I've heard about all I need to hear," shouted Chief Hightower.

Lonny and the Colonel sneered at each other across the table and grumbled underneath their breath. The Colonel removed his glasses and wiped the steam off with his handkerchief. When the chief bent down to get the keys out of the bottom drawer, Lonny surreptitiously spit out the side of his mouth and shot a stream of saliva across the desk, landing on the Colonel's shoulder. The Colonel didn't even notice. Skeeter and I both did and chuckled as Sally squeezed our hands.

"Alright," said Hightower, "There will be no charges filed regarding the fire." Then he grinned, adding, "But regarding your parole and the liquor on your breath…"

Joseph Nack walked up to the desk and placed both hands on it. "Tony, if you don't let my boy go right now, I'm gonna burn this jail to the ground myself with you and Ferny locked up in it." No one in the room doubted for a moment that Joseph's threat wasn't real. He was a man of his word, and everyone in town knew it. Ferny, once again, began to place his hand on his revolver and move in but immediately backed away just before Joseph glanced over. It was a good thing that he did, because a stupid gesture like that would have surely gotten him killed.

Hightower looked at Lonny, then over to the Colonel, and finally at Ferny. You could sense that he didn't want any part of a fight today and would rather be curled up on the couch at home watching TV. "Alright, you can go."

Sally almost jumped off the floor but remained silent. She squeezed my hand so tightly that I felt the bones crack in my fingers. The Colonel stood up, noticed something dripping down his arm, and quickly wiped off the spit with his handkerchief. That's when it hit me.

"Colonel, where's your white Bible?"

"What do you mean, son?"

"Yeah," chimed in Skeeter. "You always carry a white Bible with you."

"You had it yesterday in the alley," I added.

"I don't know. It must be at home."

Lonny picked up on where we were going with our line of questioning. "That is a bit peculiar. I don't think I've ever seen you without that white Bible." The Colonel ignored his comment and began walking toward the door when Lonny added, "Maybe we oughta check it for gasoline."

The Colonel stopped dead in his tracks. In fact, everyone in the room paused and absorbed the severity of this comment. Hightower and Ferny both raised an eyebrow and rubbed their heads. Even the stoic Joseph Nack showed an expression of surprise. There was tension on top of suspense and pressure bubbling up so high that one false move would've burst it like a balloon. Lonny strolled over behind the Colonel and stood there in silence. Even the second hand on the clock was afraid to move.

Everyone but the Colonel was focused on Lonny. He just stared at the glass pane in the door reflecting back an image of fear and maybe guilt. He didn't even notice Lonny slowly lifting his arm in the air. He only saw himself. Then with a swift blow, Lonny slapped the Colonel's back and laughed so loud that it shook the dust off a picture frame next to him. He bent over, slapped his knee, and shouted, "I really had you going, didn't I?"

We soon realized that his laughing was sincere, and it had all been a joke. Lonny continued to hoot and holler as he put a playful chokehold on the Colonel and said, "I think you shit your pants."

There were nervous laughs all around as even Chief Hightower slowly leaked out a smile. As uncomfortable as it was, it was still better than the ugly confrontation we were expecting. I don't think anyone wanted to see that outcome. Eventually, we all made it into the parking lot and said our goodbyes as Ferny drove the Colonel back home and Hightower closed up the jail for the night.

Sally invited us over for dinner, but we both politely declined, as we didn't want to be dragged into the middle of the family argument that was sure to ensue. She hugged me again and told me what a great friend I was. The smell of her skin brought back memories of lying on my bed that summer evening, and I couldn't resist stroking it one more time.

"How's everything at the shop?"

"Oh, pretty good, as long as Lonny shows up to work. Daddy's getting too old to handle it by himself all day long."

"You seeing anyone?"

"They come around, but I'm holding out for that special guy."

I didn't know how to interpret her comment. Most of the time, she was a straight shooting gal, but when it came to romance, she was just as elusive as the next girl. Now that I think about it, every woman I've ever met was an expert at guiding a conversation down a path of misinterpretation and ambiguity. I started to write a song about it one time a few years ago when I was tinkering around on the guitar. It went something like this:

"You say tomato, and I say tomahto.
You say stop, and I say go.
You know it all
And I know nothing but what you want me to know…"

That's as far as I got and you can obviously see why I never finished it. Sorry for the wandering sidebar here but, dammit, women have a tendency to do that to me and make me lose my train of thought. In fact, Sally did it to me more often than not. She was the queen of comeback lines, and I was just a pawn in this futile game of deception. I took a deep breath and replied, "I see."

Sally realized that she had me right where she wanted and asked, "How's Angie?"

"Oh, you know. It's nice but not great."

"Yeah, once you've had great, it's hard to settle for nice." And with that, she smiled and propped open the door to a plethora of options.

Joseph was leaning against the hood of the car with his keys in hand. He jiggled them a little and asked, "So Lonny, I need to know what you're gonna do here because I can't keep bailing you out of jail."

"Do how?" he asked.

"I mean this whole situation with the Colonel. You got me worried. Whatta ya plan on doing to him?"

Lonny surveyed the scene, placed his hands on the passenger side of the hood, and replied, "I'll tell you exactly what I'm going to do, Pop. I'm going to give him back his damn hat. The man has the memory of an elephant and carries a grudge longer than anyone I've ever known."

Once again, Lonny brought a smile to all our faces.

From that day forward, Lonny and Colonel Remus P. Entwhistle became the best of friends. They hung out together, walking the streets in the afternoons as the Colonel passed out discounted coupons, they drank together at Hank's Oasis, they ate off each other's plates at Buck's Diner, they shared ice cream at the Hum Dinger, and Lonny even drove Remus around to church on Sundays. That was, of course, whenever the Colonel could get Lonny out of bed on time.

We never did figure out if Lonny was sincere or just hanging with the Colonel for the amusement value. Rudy would tell us stories about seeing them up at Hank's Oasis, drinking beers, talking about politics and God. The Colonel would go off on one of his tangents, addressing the whole bar about feeling the spirit of the Lord deep inside. This was usually followed with a couple of shots of Jack Daniels and a toast by Lonny: "To the Lord, Colonel." Lonny would down his shot and say, "I feel his presence inside me now…" Then he'd grab the Colonel by the shoulders and add, "Can you feel it? I feel it. Here it comes…" Then he'd belch and say, "No, that's just indigestion."

One time, the Colonel was preaching in the park on a Sunday afternoon while a baseball tournament was going on. I was down there with Angie, watching her little brother's team trounce another in the league finals. The Colonel was walking back and forth in front of the benches, preaching his gospel as Lonny leaned back on his elbows in the second row and enjoyed the sermon. Hellfire was foaming out of the Colonel's mouth at this point with his eyes nearly bulging out of their sockets.

Lonny jumped up on his seat and yelled, "I feel it. I feel it, Colonel. I feel the Lord's presence right now. I had a dream just last night where the Lord came into my bedroom."

"God bless you, my boy. Go on." interjected the Colonel.

"There I was, standing with God in Heaven, and all around me were these clocks. There were thousands of them. Small clocks, big clocks, clocks that had names on them."

The Colonel was obviously unsure where this was going, but he nodded all the same. "Continue, my son."

"There was a clock with my name on it, and one with Hightower's name, and Fat Ferny and Alistair Dukas. Hell, everybody seemed to have a clock. I asked the Lord, I said, 'Lord, what are all these clocks for?' He looked at me and replied, 'Every man on earth has a clock, my son, and every time he jerks off, the clock moves one notch on the dial.'"

About this time, the Colonel realized that he was being duped and tried to interrupt, but Lonny was already two steps ahead of him. He leaped down, placed his hand over the Colonel's mouth and continued, "I said, 'Hallelujah, what wonderful and glorious news.' Then I looked around and asked, 'But Lord, I don't see the Colonel's clock anywhere. Where is it?' The Lord turned to me and said, 'Why, I keep it in my office and use it for a fan.'"

The crowd went wild with laughter. Several mothers stomped away in disgust with their children, but I think they did that just so they could laugh in private. The Colonel didn't talk to Lonny a whole week after that episode. But, of course, next Sunday came around, and Lonny offered to take him to church. They were back to being best friends before you knew it, and all was forgiven.

Chapter Eleven

Several fund raiser dances and auctions were held during the next few weeks to help victims of the fire. Mrs. Blanche took up residence with the Nacks since she didn't have any other family left in the area. They cleaned up and made a bedroom out of the servant's quarters on the back end of the house on the lower level. She could now watch people coming and going into the barn all day long and seemed content with the set-up. Most of the other residents found shelter in a two-story house down the street on East West Street. The owner had just converted it into apartments and, with a little financial help from the city, agreed to lodge everyone at the same rent they were paying before.

Old Man Tranchant's place was eventually sold, with the money being placed in a trust for one of the many environmental causes he so devoutly championed. It was discovered that he'd already sold much of the acreage around the farm during the last few years. Apparently, he was planning his retirement in Florida and had bought a house on the beach near Tampa Bay. The insurance company couldn't determine the cause of the fire, so they settled with the estate, leaving another sizable chunk of money to go to one of Mr. Tranchant's favorite charities. The Colonel retracted his original story and told them that he didn't see anything. A few months later, a For Sale sign appeared on the empty lot where the hardware store once sat and is still there today.

Fall rolled around and with that came football season. The Bunsen Creek Buffaloes had a decent looking team this year with T.J. playing quarterback, Buzzard in the safety position and Skeeter and me planted on the corners as wide receivers. We'd only lost one game going into the seventh week of the season, and the next game was against our neighboring archrivals, the Wingard Tigers, who were undefeated. The winner of the game would most likely go on to win the Conference.

The rivalry between towns went back to 1915 when these two coal-mining villages began to play football. Over the years, the game grew in notoriety, drawing alumni of all ages every fall. Sometime after WWII, they decided to make it official by labeling it "The Coal Bucket" game. Whoever walked away with that trophy had the inalienable right to brag all year long, and, believe me, they did.

Preparation for the big game started early Saturday morning for the Bunsen Creek High School students. Every store window downtown was painted with purple and white buffaloes colorfully obliterating orange and black tigers. Slogans like "Buffaloes Eat Tiger Meat," "Go Team Go," and "We're Number One" were plastered on the sides of buildings, benches, and cars. One student even painted a beat up old Pontiac bright purple for the occasion. At night, the teens held hands, forming human chains and paraded through the aisles of businesses chanting and singing while storeowners handed out Tootsie Pops and licorice. Then on Thursday night, to top a week of celebration, everyone gathered for a huge bonfire down at the school parking lot, complete with a full-on old-fashioned barbeque. And continuing with a tradition that went back to the beginning of the rivalry, an abandoned wooden outhouse was set ablaze and sacrificed to the Football Gods. This was no easy task by the time the '70s rolled around, as most outhouses were plowed over or converted into flower pots by then, but someone always managed to come through with the help of an unsuspecting farmer.

There was only one black kid playing football in the conference that year, and he was Wingard's star tail back, Jesse Washington, the younger brother of Leroy. No one had figured out how to stop him, and he was averaging around two hundred yards rushing per game. We had our share of black families in Bunsen Creek, but none of them seemed to have the desire to play football. I don't think it was a matter of talent. No, if you asked me, there were other elements involved here. Things just moved much slower in a small town.

Change was something you kept in your pocket and not in your mind. As I mentioned earlier, Bunsen Creek was at least ten years behind L.A. and New York when it came to fads. When it came to football, unfortunately, it was another decade or two behind that.

Since Jesse was the mayor's grandson, he received special treatment from the Wingard coaches, and it had paid off royally. They were undefeated and blowing away opponents with double digit wins every Friday night. With just a few days to go before the game, morale was low in the Buffaloes' locker room. Our coaches had scouted Wingard a couple of weeks earlier and brought in a video to watch that Sunday. By the end of the second quarter, they knew they'd made a mistake. Each Wingard lineman had a good twenty pounds on ours, and there were no flaws in Jesse's running style, no plays that were going to fool them, and no way we were going to bring the Coal Bucket back to Bunsen Creek. After practice, the four of us gathered at Skeeter's house to sulk.

T.J. was the first to start the conversation. "Holy Mary, did you see how that kid runs? He's another Gayle Sayers."

"No doubt. How are we going to stop him?" asked Skeeter.

"We could break his legs," replied Buzzard.

"Nah, that's too obvious," I said. "And, besides, Wingard would never let us get away with it without doing something to us." I turned to T.J. and added, "I mean, to you."

"True."

About that time, Skeeter's dad pulled up in his big rig and honked the horn. He'd seen the light on in the Backroom and wanted us to come outside. "Hey, look what I found in New Orleans." We ran up to the cabin as Gus jumped down and grabbed his bag. He unzipped it and pulled out a deck of cards. "No more playing poker with that scratched-up old deck."

"Gee, that's really nice, Pop," said Skeeter sarcastically.

"Well, open it up, kiddo."

Skeeter unwrapped the cards and spread them out in his hand. Lying in his palms were the prettiest naked women you'd ever seen. Redheads, blondes, tall, short, you name it. All posing in their birthday suits or hiding under the cover of a club, diamond, heart or spade.

"Wow, now that's a deck of cards," T.J. exclaimed.

"Thanks, Dad." Skeeter gave his father a hug and helped him with his bag. I think we all realized, at that moment, what a special relationship he had with his pop. Never in a million years would any of us have expected a gift like that from our fathers.

"Now don't get them all sticky and wet." Gus howled after making himself chuckle uncontrollably. When we didn't laugh back, he asked, "What's wrong with you boys? I expected to see four tally-whackers standing at attention right now."

We all sauntered up to the house with our heads down and tails tucked between our legs. When we arrived at the Backroom porch, Skeeter said, "This weekend is the Coal Bucket game, and we're going to get trounced."

Gus sat down on the porch and listened as we explained our dilemma. Retelling the story allowed us to accomplish a few things: First, it conveyed to Skeeter's dad the problem at hand. Second, it made us realize how stupid the whole thing was in the first place. Sure there were bragging rights and the taunting would be severe for a few weeks, but these things usually died down and disappeared eventually.

"I guess it's not such a big deal," I added after we finished our story.

The other guys nodded, but Gus would have nothing to do with this. "Of course, it's a big deal. Especially, if you get trounced. Let me tell you why. Later on in life, you're going to walk into a store and run into one of these football players. Believe me, the conversation will make it back to the Coal Bucket game very quick. This will stay with you forever."

"Then we're screwed," said Buzzard.

"Not exactly," Gus said slowly. He thought for a moment, then snapped his fingers. "Do you remember the story about Tom Sawyer and Huck Finn?"

We all nodded.

"Of course you do. I can't remember which one it was but remember the fence painting episode."

"It was Tom Sawyer," chimed in Buzzard, our resident keeper of useless facts.

"Well, maybe you guys need to use a little reverse psychology here."

"That's a great idea," exclaimed T.J. "We could go up to Wingard and paint the side of the high school with "Buffaloes" in real big letters."

"You're getting warmer but not quite there." Gus when on to explain a plan of attack that would have made General Patton proud. He was drawing diagrams in the dirt and digging in the basement for supplies. "Tomorrow night, you guys meet back here after dinner, and I'll make up some excuse to your parents why you have to be out late. Okay?"

Then the four of us all stretched out our right arms, held hands, and said, "To your mother."

"To your mother?" asked Gus.

"It's a long story, Dad."

"Well, some other time." He placed his hand on top of ours and repeated, "To your mother."

The next night, we met in the Backroom and played cards until about eleven o'clock. We could've gone all night with the new deck if Skeeter's dad hadn't come downstairs and knocked on the door. "It's time." Then he handed Skeeter the keys to the car. "I wish I could go with you, but I can't. Momma would tan my ass if she caught wind of this." We all understood.

We dropped off Buzzard at the dam and gave him a flashlight. He hid in the woods by the waterfall and waited for our signal. Then we drove the car around to the Leisure Club side of the lake and parked next to the railroad tracks about a half-mile away from the road, just far enough to be out of sight. We knew the trails blindfolded in that area as we'd spent many a nights camping next to the swimming pool. There were only two trailers at the campgrounds that evening and considering it was a school night, we were pretty sure that neither one was occupied. Still, we quietly snuck by and made our way along the lake until we came to the other side of the dam.

On each side of the waterfall was a wall of concrete angling down to the shores of the river below. It was thirty foot high and sixty feet wide with enough slope to support a person walking up and down it. That is, of course, as long as their feet weren't too wet from the mist coming off the dam. Skeeter flicked his flashlight on and off, signaling Buzzard on the other side. He was staked out, watching for cars coming up the dam road. One flick meant that everything was clear; two meant that someone was coming; three meant get the hell out of there as fast as you can.

We had two cans of black and orange paint, the team colors of Wingard, which Gus had purchased that day over in Indiana. It was better to be safe than sorry when it came to covering our tracks, and no one would suspect anything bought that far away. The three of us put on old painter's overalls, compliments of Gus, opened the cans up and started painting. Since we wanted it to be seen from far away, we leaned over the top of the wall and painted the first row of words upside down. They went on easily in letters four foot high. Buzzard yelled across the river, "Looks good."

The slope on the next row of words was steeper than the top, which made it harder to get into a position where you could paint. Add onto that the fact that the waterfall consistently sprayed a layer of foam on it, and we had a logistics problem. Time and time again, we kept falling and sliding down on our butts as we tried to climb the wall from the bottom.

"Dammit, what are we going to do?" asked T.J.

Skeeter wiped off his hands and searched for his paintbrush after sliding down. "We have half of it done, I'd say let's leave it at that."

"No," I said. "It won't work with just half. Let's try propping each other up."

T.J. stood on the shore and braced himself by clamping his hands on his knees. Skeeter climbed on his back, then placed his hands on the wall and said, "Alright, hop up here, Newbie."

I handed the can of paint to Skeeter, positioned my foot on T.J.'s knee and grunted, "I feel like a goddamn cheerleader." We all nearly fell into the river laughing.

"Okay, no more wisecracks. Let's get this done," T.J. ordered.

I grabbed T.J.'s shoulder and made my way up to Skeeter's belly. "Now what?" I asked.

"You're gonna have to hop up on my shoulders," replied Skeeter.

"Okay, hand me the can and brush. T.J., don't move. I'm climbing up."

"Holy Mary, we're all gonna die," he replied.

Very carefully, I moved around and propped both bare feet onto Skeeter's shoulders. I slid the handle of the paint can on my elbow, placed the brush in my mouth, and slowly stood up. Using my fingertips and the concrete for balance, I was up and ready to go. Everything was working as planned. I started painting "Buffaloes" in bold letters, starting with my left hand and switching over toward the end. Then I began the last word. The S, U, and C went on smoothly, but I found adding the last letter, was just a little bit out of my reach.

"Move farther over," I cried.

"I can't. The concrete ends here," yelled T.J.

"Crap, I'm gonna have to go on my tip toes for this one. Everyone hold on," I shouted as I searched for something solid to grasp with my other hand and leaned over. Just then, Buzzard's flashlight reflected off the white concrete. Two signals.

"Shit, hurry up. Someone's coming," cried Skeeter.

Then there was another signal. This time, it was three flashes. "I'm almost there," I said as I put the finishing touches on the K.

Now there was a set of headlights shining on us from across the river. A sudden loud beep blasted from underneath the grill of the car as Fat Ferny turned on the microphone and said, "This is the Bunsen Creek police. Stop what you're doing and put your hands in the air."

Before Ferny finished his sentence, I'd lost my footing and was sliding down the wall, paintbrush still in hand. Skeeter collapsed onto T.J. and soon we were all three sprawled out on the shoreline, caked in mud and paint.

"Let's get the hell out of here," shouted Skeeter. We left the cans and brushes behind and tore through the woods along the bank with our flashlights leading the way until a trail appeared. The dark and almost moonless night made navigating more difficult. It was hard to tell what was blood and what was orange and black paint, but we had them both running down our legs and arms. Miraculously, none of us cut open the bottom of our feet. That would've made playing on Friday almost unbearable.

I'd brought a couple of towels so we dried off at the car and removed the overalls. We pulled into the driveway, snuck into the basement to wash up, and then slipped into the Backroom through The Hole. Once we'd removed most of the paint, our wounds didn't look that bad. We sat giggling and grinning about the whole affair for another hour until there was a knock at the door.

"Oh great, Ferny tracked us down," whispered Skeeter while he turned down the light.

"Don't answer it," I whispered back.

Like three statues, we stood in total silence until a voice came from outside. "Let me in, you assholes."

"It's Buzzard," cried Skeeter.

"Of course, it's me, Ding Dong. Open the goddamn door before someone sees me."

We apologized profusely for leaving him at the dam. He forgave us and then filled us in on what had happened next. Our artwork was a near masterpiece, according to him, with the exception of the last word, which had accidentally tapered off on the end of the 'K' creating a monkey tail design that was quite stylish.

Buzzard relayed how Fat Ferny had radioed the county emergency center, which tracked down the principal of Bunsen Creek High School and got him out of bed. A few minutes later, Coach Collins showed up with the principal and surveyed the damage. The two talked for a few minutes and then went home. That's when Buzzard realized that we weren't coming to pick him up.

The next day at school, Coach Collins got on the speaker after first period and asked that all boys report to the gymnasium immediately. Rumors were already flying down the hall due to some great detective work by the office T.A. By the time the boys were lined up in single file, the whole school had heard about the paint job down at the dam. Collins ordered everyone to remove his shoes and socks, then he walked by us for inspection. We were instructed to lift our feet in the air and then extend our hands. One by one, he combed over our bodies while ignoring a constant procession of questions about what was going on. We, of course, knew what to expect the night before as Gus had instructed us to bury the overalls under the porch and soak in the bathtub scrubbing every last speck of paint away. The inspection went smoothly and nothing turned up. Skeeter was questioned about the scratches on his arms but quickly contributed them to a tussle he'd gotten into with the neighbor's cat. The coach lectured us for fifteen minutes about childish behavior and how we were all going to Hell until his dentures flew out of his mouth and slid across the gymnasium floor.

An inspection went on at Wingard High and ended with the same results. That, of course, didn't relieve them of any suspicion. At lunchtime, every car in the parking lot was gone and congregating down at the dam to see the damage. There it was, in bold orange and black letters. The only words in the English language vengeful enough to ignite a force so powerful that it would all but guarantee a victory on Friday night: "Tigers Rule, Buffaloes Suck."

There are no amount of words that can fully describe just how pissed off the football players were over this little prank. More helmets were cracked and shoulder pads unhinged those next two days at practice than during the whole rest of the season combined. The coach barely let us onto the field the day before the game because two backup players had already suffered concussions. Every parking spot around the football field was occupied the night before, and people had already staked out chairs along the sidelines and around the goal posts. By the time Friday night rolled around, the stadium was jam packed before suppertime.

We knocked their star running back out of the game before the second quarter ended. The referees ejected one of our linebackers and coaches after they argued a late hit penalty but that only sparked the team to be even more aggressive. T.J. threw four touchdown passes to Skeeter and me. Even Buzzard had an interception by the time the game was through. Ambulances from neighboring towns were called in after two other Wingard players went down. The coach tried to take control and calm everyone at half time, reminding them that we were ahead by twenty-four points, but it did no good. The carnage kept falling as the points climbed. By the mid-third quarter, Wingard had taken out all of their first stringers and replaced them with the second team.

When we gathered back at Skeeter's house later that night, his dad couldn't stop giggling and prancing around on the porch. There were so many high fives going around that my hands were calloused. Even mean-old Charlie Springer came out of his rat hole to enjoy the festivities. He wouldn't smile or say anything but just walked up and down Main Street for hours with his fist clenched and stretched high into the air.

Yes, we were running on all four that night and raising hell. The hair on our necks had stood up and sprung into action. We were a pack of wolves who'd just circled our prey, a pride of lions that had just outrun a herd of antelope, a group of boys that had just tasted manhood. It was brief, and maybe that's best, but it was a defining moment at that. A moment we'd rarely seen in our normal daily lives. A moment I will cherish forever.

We never did tell anyone about the ordeal. It would have ruined the whole mystique surrounding the legend that grew in size every day thereafter. Besides, no one would have believed us. Only Fat Ferny had a clue about what really happened a few weeks later when he noticed an orange splotch on one of Skeeter's tires. He just shook his head and drove off.

This wasn't the only secret we vowed to keep. No there were others, some so small that I've forgotten them already, others that I'll never forget. But we aren't there quite yet so I'll save that story for later.

ACT testing came and went that fall, prompting everyone to start thinking about graduation, college, and beyond. Buzzard and I had already made up our minds to go, but Skeeter and T.J. had other plans. We tried everything to convince them but they just weren't interested in dormitories, fraternities, or hot chicks from Chicago. Skeeter had already lined up a job after graduating at General Motors through his neighbor, and T.J. had decided to spend the next few years working in the coal mines out west of town. The salaries were unbelievably good for kids right out of high school, and they figured they could save enough money in five years to buy a house.

"Come on, Newbie," T.J. said one night as we walked home together. "My dad can get us both a job out there through his brother. Five years in the mines won't kill you. Then you'd have enough money to go to any college you wanted to, maybe even Harvard."

"I don't think Harvard wants me. Maybe Buzzard, but I'm not Ivy League material."

"Still, you could write your own ticket. It beats going to junior college."

"What makes you think I'm going to junior college?"

"Well, how else are you going to pay for the U of I? I mean, Buzzard's dad owns a business and all, so he's set. You have...oh, never mind."

T.J. stopped short of saying the obvious. There was no way my dad could afford to send me to a four-year school like Buzzard's. His older sister was graduating from the University of Illinois that spring. After spending a *Lost Weekend* with her over Halloween and seeing how cool college life was, he'd set his sights on following in her footsteps.

A part of me wanted to go there too. It was just far enough away to get into all kinds of trouble but not so far that you couldn't be bailed out if need be. Unfortunately, my grades were just good enough to get me in but not good enough to qualify for any major scholarships. That meant either financial aid or one heck of a good paying job...like coal mining. The thought of graduating was now starting to bring me down. There was also the issue of leaving my pop all alone. He hadn't dated since mother died and that had to be affecting him emotionally, if not physically. When he wasn't out collecting insurance payments, he'd come home at night, eat a TV dinner, and watch the boob tube until he fell asleep on the couch. Somehow, his life seemed so meaningless these last few years. I'm sure I was responsible for part of that, considering we hardly talked about anything other than sports. Still, I didn't know what to do.

Angie, on the other hand, had her heart set on attending an Ivy League school. We entertained each other with fairytale stories and shallow commitments about marrying after college but neither one of us, I don't think, thought it would ever happen. Her father was barely hanging onto the discount store business and the fights between her parents were more frequent and much louder. They didn't seem to care whether we heard them or not anymore. We spent most of the time taking long walks down the aisles of the store and carrying on romantic conversations on the front steps in order to avoid the mayhem. When the occasional customer did come in, Angie loved to mock them behind their backs while I catered to their every whim, trying to make a sale. She didn't care what happened to her father's business. When she finished school, she had plans to live in New York and become an actress.

Everyone loved the winter snow and cold for the first few months, right up to Christmas time. After the holidays, the gloomy, sunless skies settled in over the prairie and didn't leave until April. Life could be unbearable during that time of year. I don't have any raw data or official surveys to back it up, but I'd bet more people thought about committing suicide during those few months than any other part of the year. By the time spring rolled around, people were smiling again and coming out of hibernation.

A storm front had moved in on the first day of May and hovered around for four days, dumping so much rain that most back yards looked like mud ponds. It had also soaked the dirt fields so badly that the farmers had no choice but to sit up at Buck's Diner and sip coffee all day. They couldn't finish a conversation without adding in the words, "bad harvest."

I went down to Bunsen Creek behind the house to see how high the water had risen. Sporting knee-high rubber boots and overalls, I did my best not to slide all the way down the hill. The normally peaceful meandering stream had been transformed into a raging river. Hundred-year-old hollowed out trees had been uprooted during the storms and were now settling into their final resting place across the valley floor. Some of the branches had been submerged under the rapidly flowing water just enough to create a series of white caps and frothing whirlpools. Aromas of coal dust and dormant microbes, unearthed for the first time in centuries, filtered through the misty air. The woods were bustling with unfamiliar noises today as all forms of wildlife, normally hidden from the elements, were out in abundance, jockeying for position in the new world order that always emerges after such a storm.

I stood there on the newly formed banks of the flowing stream and watched nature take its course. *God's Country indeed*, I thought. Even after man's brutal attempt to destroy its beauty by stripping coal out of the ground and leaving it barren, the landscape had recovered and thrived once more. Yet, as I felt the forest breathing again and brushing off the damage caused by a few humans years before, I couldn't help but wonder how many more times it could survive these intrusions in the years to come.

I tried to picture my mom and dad decades earlier frolicking through the brush without a care in the world. Humming along and thinking only about the moment, with no worries, no choices, and no consequences. I wondered at what point in a person's life does that concept vanish forever. Once you've experienced a few of life's tragedies, can you ever get that lighthearted feeling back? I honestly don't think so. And, right then, with only a few months of school left and so many decisions to be made, the only thing I felt was confusion. There were no images of Mother in a summer dress that day.

As I walked back up the hill, I noticed a sign over on the other bank. I squinted hard in order to read the words "Private Property." Now Old Man Tranchant was known for running off hunters, but no way would he ever post a sign telling people to keep out. Curiosity got the best of me so I took a detour across the embankment using one of the newly formed tree bridges dangling over the stream. I could hear chainsaws in the distance as I made my way to the top. The farmhouse was barely visible through the trees but I could clearly see a "For Sale" sign near the road with a "Sold" sticker slapped across it. When I turned to head back, I spotted another one down about a quarter of a mile. Apparently, the estate had finally sold off the rest of his land. And with that, just like the storm that had come through earlier rearranging the landscape, one generation had been erased from memory and another had appeared.

Chapter Twelve

When the end of the school year was almost upon us, we decided that it was a perfect time to go ghost hunting. Even though Halloween had come and gone, scaring the pants off a few gullible girls, figuratively and most sincerely, sounded better than anything else we could come up with. Skeeter still had his werewolf mask in the trunk of his car, so he left an hour earlier and hid out east of town next to the old abandoned cemetery. The rest of us picked up Angie and the Foster twins then headed out for a night of entertainment. Buzzard wove together a tale about death, severed arms, flashing lanterns in the night, and lost souls on the way there. By the time we arrived, he had me shaking.

We pulled in and turned the lights out on the car. He guided it to the back of the cemetery where a headstone more than a hundred years old was lying. Everyone got out of the car and turned on their flashlights. You could barely read the writing on most tombstones so you had to get close with your light. Every once in a while, someone would say, "What was that?" or "Did something move over there?" A pair of hound dogs howling somewhere far away echoed in the air. It was so befitting for the occasion, almost as if we'd cued them up like some haunting amusement park ride. Even though we couldn't see the actual farmhouse, we knew it was there down the road. Completely out of sight and just out of shouting distance.

"Here it is," shouted T.J. "Over here."

As we all snuggled up around the gravesite, I brushed off the limestone and read the inscription, "You may feel brave now here with your friends, till I follow you home when the night ends."

"I'm scared. Let's get back to the car," whimpered one of the Foster twins. We all piled in as Buzzard threw the car into gear and started up the gravel road. Just before we made it to the gate, the headlights reflected off a man standing in front of a tombstone with his back turned to us.

Good, here's Skeeter. This should be fun, I thought.

When the man spun around, he was wearing the werewolf mask and holding a bloody machete in his hand. That's when we noticed Skeeter's motionless body propped up against the tombstone behind him. His eyes were wide open, staring off into the Milky Way above as if searching for a place to lay his soul to rest. Blood dripped from his forehead, which now more resembled the top of an open paint can than a human skull. Gashes in his shirt were caked in red and brown, exposing open wounds.

The man hobbled onto the gravel road and blocked our escape. We could hear him growl under the mask as he slowly approached the vehicle. Buzzard's hands were frozen on the steering wheel. I could tell that he was having trouble comprehending what was taking place and not sure what to do next. The girls' screams swirled around and filled our minds with even more uncertainty. Could Skeeter's prank have gone so terribly wrong or should we still play along?

Before he had time to act, the man pounded on the hood and began circling the car. He was yelling, "Come out, come out and play," repeatedly while jumping up and down.

"What do I do, Newbie?"

It was then that I realized my hand was squeezing the top of the back seat so hard that the seams had ripped open. My other arm was being yanked out of its socket by Angie as she tried to claw her way under my jacket. Just then, I saw Skeeter's eyes glance over at the car. Then the corner of his lip curled up ever so slightly.

"You dog," I murmured.

Buzzard's eyes were glaring back at me in the rear view mirror waiting for a response. I winked and said, "Let's get out and help Skeeter."

With that, we jumped out the car and ran over to the tombstone. The man, who'd now developed a limp, dragged himself in our direction moaning and laughing at the same time.

"Boy, I hope you're right about this," spouted T.J.

"Get off my leg, idiot," whispered Skeeter as he indiscreetly kicked Buzzard.

We both let out a deep sigh and kept playing along. The man was within ten feet now, still lugging one leg across the grass. He raised the machete into the air and calmly asked, "How am I doin', boys?" As his plastic machete chopped at us until we were all lifelessly lying on the ground. I couldn't help from snorting incessantly.

"Oh, you want more," shouted the man. He grabbed my legs and pulled me through the wet grass over to another grave marker. Right then, one of the Foster twins in the front seat slid over behind the wheel and put the car into gear.

"Holy crap," yelled Buzzard as he jumped up and ran toward the vehicle. The tires were spewing mud and gravel as it gained momentum. "Stop! It's just a joke."

We were all up on our feet by then. The man in the mask lifted it off his head and said, "April Fools. Well, maybe a little belated, but close enough." It was Lonny. The car slammed on its brakes after seeing Buzzard. Then the girl in the front seat jumped out, stomped over to him, and started swinging wildly. "You scared the daylights out of me," she squawked.

"Hey, don't have a cow. I didn't know all this was happening," replied Buzzard as he grabbed each arm and tried to restrain her.

"Ah man, that was the best ghost-hunting prank ever," boasted Skeeter as he high-fived Lonny.

"No kidding. You had us all crapping our pants. Did you two plan this?" I asked.

"No, I got here about an hour ago, and Lonny spotted my car. I told him what I was doing and, well, he decided to help."

"It's the least I could do. I mean, what's the fun in just scaring a couple of girls? Hell, I can do that by just riding my horse around town. But watching a few growing boys freak out, now that's a different story. I feel like Lon Chaney Jr. tonight," and with that, Lonny howled at the moon. He definitely wasn't walking on two feet that night.

"You could've given me a heart attack," exclaimed Angie, who'd finally gathered up enough courage to get out of the back seat. She squeezed my arm and tried to hide under my jacket.

"Hey, you lived, didn't ya? No blood, no foul, right?" noted Lonny.

The girls looked at each other and repeated, "No blood, no foul?"

There it was again: Lonny's favorite saying, his motto, his maxim, his *obiter dictum* for how a person should live their life. I realized, at that moment, that he didn't just say it to diffuse the tension. No, it was much more: This *WAS* his life. This is how he lived every day. This is what gave his existence meaning. He had a life with purpose. As I came to this conclusion, all I could think about was: What was mine?

Angie nodded and chuckled. "I don't know about blood, but I definitely peed my pants tonight." That comment made us all wet our pants.

"Well everyone, I have to be going. I was supposed to pick up the Colonel an hour ago. We have some important business to tend to."

"Thanks, Lonny," I said. "You were amazing." And with that, he winked and disappeared into the darkness.

We drove around for another two hours that night, blindly navigating the countryside with no map. Our car followed the road as far as it would go, occasionally, slipping in and out of small villages along the way. Many of them were so remote that they didn't even have street signs. Sometimes, there'd be an intersection with a neon-lit gas station lurking in the shadows of a single streetlight. But they were always closed for the night and probably forever as far as we could tell.

My mind kept drifting as we meandered from one gravel road to the next. Seeing Lonny running around in that werewolf mask, the spastic eye movements, the howling at the moon all seemed to be so fitting. He was definitely in his element. As the hours ticked away, I wondered if he really was going through a transformation of his own. Maybe he was just transitioning from a boy to a man; maybe that animalistic urge inside had finally overtaken any desire to remain a normal human being, or maybe it was something deeper and darker that I hadn't even thought of yet.

On the way back into town, there were vehicles parked three deep at the square. People were sitting on the hoods of cars talking while others bounced around from car to car. What was even more odd was that there was no sign of Hightower's police car anywhere. He would've normally been all over this scene, flashing lights and barking out orders.

"Pull in," I said.

Buzzard cruised over to Mary Makowski's car and asked, "What the heck's going on?"

"Down at the dam, there's been a wreck."

"A wreck. Who?"

"I heard it was Lonny Nack. Sounds like it's really bad too." Mary peered over at me in the back seat and in a somber tone added, "Sorry Newbie."

"No way, we just saw him a couple of hours ago," chimed in T.J.

I froze for a moment letting this all sink in. Angie rubbed my hand and attempted to console me as best as she could. It was useless. I took a deep breath, let it out, and said to the Foster twins, "Girls, can we let you off here to find a ride home? We need to go check this out."

"I'll give them a ride," offered Mary. I half-smiled and thanked her as they filed out of the car and said their goodbyes.

Skeeter hopped in with us, and Buzzard threw the car into gear, speeding off toward the dam. On the drive there, no one said a word. I mean, what could you say? I tried to remain calm and hopeful, but so many different thoughts and scenarios kept running through my brain. Knowing Lonny, it was probably just another one of his pranks. There was also a good chance that it wasn't as bad as Mary had heard. After all, these types of rumors did have a tendency to run wild. But wedged in the back of my mind was the possibility that this time his luck had really run out.

When we'd made it halfway down the Old Dam Road, we saw the flashing lights of the Wingard police car. They'd barricaded the turn off to the dam and were stopping every vehicle that tried to pass.

Buzzard pulled over by the bridge, and we walked the rest of the way up. Alistair Dukas's house was on the corner, and every light was on. I saw Mrs. Dukas on the porch with a few people sitting on the steps.

Angie saw her and ran over as we crossed into their yard.

"What happened?" she cried.

"There was a two-car wreck down at the cove. Lonny Nack and Officer Hightower's cars."

"How bad is it?"

"I don't know. The ambulance went down there a minute ago but nobody's come up yet. I think Alistair's down there now."

I noticed the Colonel sitting in the back seat of a police car with the door open holding an ice pack on his head. "Was he involved?"

"Yeah, he came up to the door a few minutes ago and asked me to call for an ambulance."

The four of us marched over to the police car while Angie remained behind with her mother. The Colonel was by himself as the cops were busy directing traffic. He saw us coming and said, "Hello, boys."

"Colonel, what happened?"

He looked from side to side to make sure that none of the cops were listening in, and then whispered, "Hightower was chasing us all over the county. Lonny stole this farmer's pig and was going to barbeque it for Sunday dinner. We were going to invite the whole congregation over. The farmer saw us leave and called it in. The next thing I know, Hightower was following us on Peabody Road. Lonny hightailed it down south and then cut across a country road heading toward Elmwood Grove. We lost the pig out the back of the truck on the big turn doing seventy miles an hour." He shook his head and sighed. "Oh my, how that pig did fly. Poor thing."

After wiping his forehead, he continued, "Then Lonny gunned it on Route 1 heading back toward town when Hightower caught up to us. We turned on the Old Dam Road and headed for the lake, thinking we could lose him around the turn and duck down into the woods. Then, all of a sudden, Bobby McIntosh came out of nowhere with a fishing pole in his hand. Lonny tried his best to avoid hitting him, but it was too late. Lonny's truck started doing somersaults and headed right for the cove. By the time we'd stopped rolling, the truck was sitting halfway in the water on its side. Lonny was pinned in under the steering wheel and said his legs felt broken. I was able to slip out of the window and get to my feet. He told me to go get help so I went over to Hightower's car to use the radio. The Chief was unconscious, but he was still breathing. His radio was dead, and when he started to moan, I thought it best just to get the hell out of there before he woke up. Then I ran down the road to Dukas's and called for an ambulance. And here I am."

"Lonny's okay though?" I asked.

The Colonel just shrugged and said, "Yeah, he seemed fine, but that truck was just barely hanging on the edge of the cove."

Sally and her father drove up and parked in Angie's front yard. A Wingard cop came over to talk to them both. He pointed over to the Colonel and explained the situation. Joseph was visibly upset at the man and yelling in his ear. Sally peered over and made eye contact.

"I'll be back," I said before running over to her side. "Any word?"

"No, this goon won't let us go down there to see how Lonny is."

There wasn't really anything else to say, so I grabbed her hand and held on tightly.

The officer got on the car radio, then came back, and said, "It's okay for you to go down there now."

"Thank you," replied Joseph. He hopped in the car and looked to Sally. "Let's go."

She yanked on my arm and said, "Come with me."

I opened her door and started to get in when the cop stopped me. "Hold on. It's just family."

"Back off, officer. He's with us," shouted Joseph.

The cop raised his arms in the air and stepped back. Joseph threw the car into gear and raced down the gravel road. It was just a few hundred yards to the turn, and we were there in seconds. There was an ambulance next to the police car and another one just arriving. The paramedics had Bobby on a gurney and were loading him into the back of the ambulance. A white sheet completely covered his body. They tossed his mangled fishing pole into the cab, turned on the siren, and sped off.

Fat Ferny and Alistair Dukas were standing next to Hightower who was receiving first aid from a medic. Joseph took one look and walked right passed them toward the cove. Lonny's truck was almost submerged underwater with only the back of the bed showing. The rains that spring had raised the water level at the dam to a near-record high. We watched as the other medic and fireman tied a chain around the cab and secured it to the back of the fire truck. The only illumination came from the glow of a full moon and the ambulance's headlights as the light pole had been knocked over completely.

"Go ahead and pull," one of them yelled.

The fire truck slowly flipped the Chevy over and back onto dry ground. Water and mud seeped out through the cracks around the doors. The top of the cab had been rolled so many times that every window including the windshield was completely gone.

Everyone rushed over and watched the fireman use a device to remove the steering wheel and free Lonny's body. As they lifted him out of the cab, his legs dangled precariously while they dragged him onto the grass. The medic laid him down on his back and checked his vital signs. His eyes were wide open and lifeless. Water drops rolled off his naked torso, and his soaked blue jeans were torn from the kneecaps down. Besides a few scratches on his cheeks and chest, his body was clean of any wounds.

Sally ran over and pushed the medic aside. "Get away from him." She brushed away the mud from his face and shouted, "Lonny, wake up! Wake up!"

Her father leaned over and placed his hand on her shoulder. "He's gone, Sally. Let it be." On the other side of the cove, somewhere hidden in the woods, a herd of wild cats mourned the loss with a solemn chorus of meows and moans. When I looked over, all I saw were fireflies blinking around a few slanted eyes reflecting off the flashing red lights.

Sally wrapped her arms around her brother and sobbed quietly for what seemed to be an eternity. No one dared to interrupt her. I just stared in disbelief. It had all the makings of one of those surreal bad dreams you hear about, and I wanted to pinch myself to see if this was actually happening, but I knew my senses were already numb. Joseph's glazed eyes glanced over for a moment then looked away. The last time I'd seen a grown man cry was my own father that tragic day a few years before.

Another emergency vehicle soon pulled up with its headlights blanketing the scene. Sally's shadow stretched over the water and into the treeline, still hiding her grief. She raised her head, brushed away the tears, and stared back at the light in defiance. I walked over and whispered, "They need to do their jobs, Sally."

She nodded and stood up, letting Lonny's hand drop into the mud. The light beams exposed a new tattoo on his arm. It looked like Latin writing, which I found to be odd. There were just two words, "Carpe Diem."

Sally turned away and began sobbing again when she noticed the markings. I whispered in her ear, "What does it mean?"

She took a deep breath and let it out before replying, "Seize the Day."

"Of course."

As they lifted his body on a gurney and pushed it up the hill, Chief Hightower walked over and watched them place it into the ambulance. He didn't say a word as his swollen lip and bloodied forehead flaunted the good fortune he'd experienced that night. He'd drawn the long straw and was going home alive instead of riding to the morgue. Yet, when he glanced over, I swear I saw him sneer. Underneath his somber, thick-skinned carcass was a soulless man jumping for joy. His prayers had finally been answered.

I remembered what the Colonel had said about Lonny asking him to go get help. He was alive and conscious when Remus left, and now his white lifeless corpse was being placed in a body bag. The only other witness was standing next to the ambulance, playing the role of Chief again. With one arm in a sling, standing like Napoleon posing for a portrait, he ordered Ferny to help with the body. Something was definitely wrong with this picture.

As Lonny's shirtless body was lifted into the vehicle, I noticed that there wasn't any blood. "No blood, no foul," I whispered to myself. Those words had been Lonny's mantra in life. His way of apologizing without actually saying, "I'm sorry." I could sense that his spirit was whispering those words into Sally's and her father's ears right then and there. Somewhere in that darkened space between worlds, where Heaven and Hell lies, he was asking for forgiveness one last time. He'd let them down again, and there was no way he was going to be able to fix this one. As the feline moans haunted the woods in the background, those four words lingered in the air.

Both Hightower and the Colonel were taken up to Kickapoo County Hospital for observation and a few x-rays. They were released the next morning, and no charges were filed against the Colonel since he was just the passenger in the vehicle. I couldn't help but think this was all part of a plea deal in return for his silence on the matter of Lonny's appearance when he left the scene of the crime. Of course, I couldn't prove any of this.

A copy of the police and coroner's reports arrived at the funeral home about ten minutes before the services started. It was determined that Lonny died from drowning as his lungs were full of water. There were no other external wounds found on the victim except for a few bruises where his chest had been pinned in under the steering wheel. Both his legs were broken. They estimated the speed with which he hit Bobby McIntosh to be approximately sixty-five miles an hour, a good forty miles over the speed limit. Even without the soggy weather conditions, the chances of him dodging the boy and making that turn were slim.

By the time Joseph got around to reading the report, Lonny was six feet underground. So many people attended the service that the funeral director had to open up the annex in order to accommodate them all. Everyone came to pay their last respects: friends, neighbors, loyal customers, and people who hardly even knew the man. Say what you want about him, no one could dispute the fact that he'd touched more souls in his lifetime than all of us combined.

There was an old custom in the Nack family that dated back hundreds of years where each attendee at the funeral service was asked to place an item in the casket to be buried with the deceased. This Indian tradition would ward off evil spirits and help protect the soul in the afterlife. There were old photos, hand-written notes, beer cans, and cigarettes strewn around Lonny's rigid body everywhere.

Charlie Springer, who'd taken the time out of his busy schedule of annoying Alistair Dukas and terrorizing the folks up at city hall, shuffled in and laid the Purple Heart he'd won in the First World War on top of Lonny's chest.

When the four of us ambled up to the casket, T.J. grabbed my arm and whispered, "That's my freaking jacket on him."

"I can see that."

"I thought you said it was at the dry cleaners."

I slipped the harmonica Lonny had given me under his left hand. I figured that he might very well need it to serenade an angel or two in order to get into Heaven. "Well, I lied. What do you want me to do? Take it off of him?"

Just then, Sally walked up to T.J. and kissed him on the cheek. "Thank you so much for giving Lonny your extra suit. Newbie told me all about it."

T.J., who'd turned whiter than his dress shirt, mumbled a few syllables before saying, "Yeah, well, you know…"

I couldn't resist the temptation and interjected, "…Sally, what he's really trying to say is that—"

"It's an honor to have Lonny buried in my suit," blurted T.J.

Skeeter and Buzzard could barely hold in the laughter as we slowly moved on and found our seats. The funeral was short and sweet, just like Lonny would've wanted it. The Colonel gave a rousing eulogy for his best friend and handled all the prayers and quotes from scripture. When Alice Cooper's "Eighteen" came on the loudspeakers as the crowd started exiting, everyone in the audience chuckled. That started an avalanche of discussions about what was the funniest shenanigan Lonny had ever pulled off.

After we buried him, the crowd headed out to the Nacks' for refreshments and the stories continued there until the wee hours of the night. Hank's Oasis furnished a free keg of beer and Mrs. Blanche made potato salad, green beans and fried chicken. She'd lost a good hundred pounds since moving in with the Nacks and was able to move around without a cane on most days.

The four of us sat right next to the keg and, thankfully, no one was keeping score on who was drinking and who wasn't. We were almost daring the police to show up and stop the party. The conversation eventually made it back to what we were going to do after high school. Skeeter and T.J. reconfirmed their plans, and Buzzard revealed that he'd been accepted into the U of I.

"What are you going to do, Newbie?" he asked.

"I don't know. I'm not sure. I got into the U of I, but there's the whole money issue."

"I can still get you the job out at the coal mine, but don't wait too long. My uncle said he can't hold it forever."

"Understood."

Buzzard raised his cup and said, "Dude, go in debt with me at the U of I, and we'll both meet up here four years from now and panhandle on the square together."

"To your mother," I replied.

Then we all raised our cups. "To your mother."

The Colonel had been avoiding us the whole evening. We hadn't spoken to him since the night of the crash. He'd visited with almost everyone else by the time he inadvertently ended up in front of our table. No doubt, he wanted to make sure he was good and liquored up before talking with us.

"Have a seat, Colonel," beckoned Skeeter.

The Colonel whipped around and almost lost his hat when he realized who'd spoken to him. The magnified lenses in his glasses made his dilated pupils look like M&Ms against the black frames on his nose. His seersucker suit had grass stains on the elbows and knees, probably the result of a disastrous attempt to dance the polka with one of Sally's cousins earlier in the evening. He filled up his plastic cup, plopped into a fold out chair, and snorted, "A seat it 'tis." His head swayed back from Skeeter to T.J. to Buzzard before finally settling on me. "Ah yes, the Fearsome Foursome, the Four Horsemen, the Bunsen Creek Quartet." He pushed his frames up off the end of his nose. "What can I do you for, gentlemen?"

"That was a great speech you gave at the funeral," said T.J. "It really came from the heart."

"Why thank you there, young fellow. I am proud to have been his dear friend." The last word was almost inaudible as he gulped down another swig.

I looked over to Sally, who was numbly standing next to her aunt, acting like she was interested in what she was saying. It was obvious that her mind was a million miles away. Her father had been evading most visitors all evening long by hiding out in the barn. I'd seen him earlier, standing in the shadows smoking a cigarette.

I finished my beer and said, "So Colonel, the coroner's report says that Lonny died from drowning. That seems to contradict your story."

"I know what I saw, and I know what I didn't see. Lonny was alive when I left for help. I swear on a stack of Bibles."

"What do you think happened?"

The Colonel shook his head. "I don't know. The truck was close to the edge of the water, but I managed to get out without it tipping over."

"So what are you saying?"

The Colonel tightened up his shoulders and leaned in over the table. He motioned everyone to do likewise, while scanning the area just to make sure nobody else was around. Then he said, "I'm saying, off the record, and if anyone calls me to testify, I will deny ever having this conversation, but Officer Hightower had something to do with this."

"You think Hightower pushed the truck in?" asked Buzzard.

The Colonel just nodded repeatedly. I was waiting for him to fall asleep into his cup like a bobbing drinking bird, but, at the last second, he surprised us all by perking up and shouting, "Another drink?"

He got his second wind and went off on a long dissertation about the lessons learned and taught by Lonny. I must admit, the man could tell a story, but my mind was elsewhere. I couldn't keep my eyes off Sally. Finally, between sips of beer, I excused myself and walked over to where she was standing. She welcomed the opportunity to break away from her relatives and asked me to take a walk with her.

"Rough night?"

"Is it ever," she replied. "I just can't get him out of my mind, Newbie. I mean, he was my only brother. What am I going to do now?"

"Well, you still got the shop, and now there's Mrs. Blanche."

She smiled at that comment. "That's almost funny. Yeah, another mouth to feed. That's exactly what I need."

I grabbed her hand and said, "I know that you have the weight of the world on your shoulders, right now. And I know what it's like to lose a family member. But you know, it too will pass."

"I know," she said while she squeezed my hand. "I just don't know how long I can hold out. Lonny was the glue that held everything together. Daddy was counting on him to take over and, Lord knows, I can't run the place."

"Well, maybe you should sell it. Take the money and go to school or something."

"I can't do that to Daddy. He'd be lost without the store."

She stopped me when we'd reached the tree line by the railroad tracks. "Newbie, you were the first, you know. There's always going to be a special place in my heart for you."

"Me too."

"I wish life could always stay that innocent and easy. I don't want to grow up or leave town or have to make these kinds of decisions."

"I know. A part of me doesn't want to grow up either. Especially, if it means breaking up the gang and all."

"At least you have them. I have an old man, a fat lady with a cat that's half the size of a horse...and a horse!"

We both smiled and stared at each other for a few minutes. Even though our relationship had taken a detour, there was still a strong connection. A part of me wanted to grab her and kiss her until my lips fell off, but I didn't. We talked for a long time. I felt like I could tell her anything, and I think she felt the same. In another place and time, we could've been just right for each other, but not tonight.

You know, Mother Nature has a peculiar way of dealing with humans. Timing is everything, and women's biological clocks always seemed to be out of sync with men's. Yet, can we blame everything bad that happens on Mother Nature and everything good on God himself? Can it really be that simple? The Colonel's sermon about God's little plan for Lonny sounded good at the funeral home, but right now, it did little to quench my thirst for answers. Yes, life was unfair. To me, that's all anyone had to say about the matter. There are those who were born lucky and those not so lucky—and then there were others like me, somewhere in between.

Chapter Thirteen

Senior year was in full swing, and even though our sights were set on making it the best one of our lives, we hadn't forgotten about Hightower. The four of us made a pact that before graduating, we were going to get the chief fired and link him to Lonny's murder in some way. Now all we had to do was figure out how. We'd already taken every "For Sale" sign in town and mounted them into Hightower's front yard. They were placed in rows like tombstones, which illustrated the exact visual effect we were going for. Just to make sure our point was made, R.I.P. was painted on the ones in the front. Then, to top it off, we placed an anonymous call to the mayor's office telling him that there were strange and morbid things going on at the chief's house. That was Buzzard's idea, of course, granny voice and all.

As the leaves turned color and wilted away, so did our hopes of linking Hightower to the murder. It was one man's word against another's, and neither one was speaking. The State's Attorney's office was looking into the deaths as part of a routine investigation. Lonny's death had been ruled a case of negligence on the part of the victim, but the fisherman who died was a completely different story. Hightower was questioned as to why such a high-speed chase was warranted, considering the only crime committed was the alleged theft of a pig. He'd been put on a paid leave of absence while the investigation continued.

With the change in weather, came the fall cleaning ritual at home. Once again, I was ordered to spruce up the house and clear out the brush on the hillside before the snow fell. Over the years, our back yard had gained notoriety as having the best snow sledding in town.

The slope was perfect for a good, long run all the way down to the creek. After the removal of any shrubs or fallen trees that might obstruct the path, you were ready for business. With the heavy rains last spring, there were plenty of obstacles to be moved.

A cool breeze swirled through the valley that morning. I zipped my jacket up and braced for the worst. What leaves that were left on the tree branches were quickly losing any hope of lasting another day. I called out to Mother, just to see if she'd respond. It had been a while since my last encounter, and I'd all but given up on making contact. I stood there for a few minutes and heard nothing. It was no use.

Then the wind limbered up again, causing the branches to moan and stretch downward. I could feel the icy chill of winter awakening and cleansing my face. A piece of cloth floated by and latched onto a limb. It was faded and torn, but hints of green and yellow flickered around the stitching as it flapped in the breeze.

"Go away," the air hissed, followed by a gust of misty vapor.

"Mother, is that you?"

Then another sound echoed by me and lingered. "Go…"

 "Where are you?"

And with that, the cloth disappeared into the bushes. I ran over to investigate but found nothing. Even the wind was shrouded in silence now. I covered every foot of that hillside, searching and hoping she'd return, but to no avail. Soon I found myself back on the sledding trail. A half hour wasted, and I was no closer to finishing my chores.

Oh well, I said to myself. *Maybe it's better this way.*

I began clearing away the brush, moving boulders and chunks of rotted wood to the side. It was tedious work. As I dragged a limb off the path, a sharp pain pricked the back of my neck. By the time I'd reached up to feel it, something else had hit me on the shoulder. I looked up and there was Billy Hightower with his little brother, Jerry, laughing in their back yard.

"Cut it out, dork," I yelled.

"Make me, punk."

"Come on down here, then."

As the two brothers skidded through the mud and undergrowth, I clenched my fists ready to do battle. Visions of Sally being tormented and abused by Billy's gang flashed across the hillside as I stood my ground. I could see his little brother's hand covering her mouth as the other two held her down. Her screams muffled like the shuffling leaves muting their footsteps. By the time he'd made it down the hill, I was already swinging.

The first punch caught him off guard and landed solidly on his chin. He fell back into his brother's arms and immediately retaliated. I dodged a few blows before his brother suckerpunched me in the gut. As I dropped my arm to protect my abdomen, Billy's fist plowed into my left jaw, sending me back against a tree. For a moment, my vision blurred, causing me to feel disoriented. I instinctively kicked as hard as I could, hoping to connect with anything. My leg jolted up wildly and missed, but it made them back up a step, which allowed me just enough time to get my bearings.

We danced around in a circle with our fists ready, waiting for the other person to make the next move. I focused on Billy's eyes with pinpoint accuracy while keeping his brother in my peripheral vision. Every few steps, someone would flinch and try to provoke the other into a compromising position.

"I know what you did to Sally, you bastard." I blurted without even realizing what I'd said. I could tell that he was absolutely flabbergasted by the remark.

Jerry was even more shocked and cried, "I told you that it'd come back and bite you on the ass."

"Shut up!" he snarled. Then he glared at me and added, "She had it coming. And besides, there's not a damn thing you can do about it, punk."

"If he knows, then anyone could know," whined his little brother as he lowered his hands. Before either one could react, I planted a left hook on the side of Jerry's head. He went down cold.

Billy caught me in the right eye with a weak left jab, but it was enough to make me lose my balance. The next thing I knew, my legs were sinking into the ground. The dirt had given out around me, exposing a gaping hole. As the earth swallowed everything underneath me, I frantically grasped for anything solid to hold onto. I could hear rocks and dirt clogs bouncing off sheet metal below.

My fingers continued sifting through the mud until they finally connected with something solid. When the rubble ceased tumbling down, I was hanging on for dear life with both hands tightly choking a single tree root.

"Billy, give me a hand." He was tending to his little brother, who was unconscious and lying on his side a few feet away. He ignored my cries until I shouted again. "Billy, help me."

When he looked up, I knew I was in trouble. I'd witnessed that same gaze on the playground years ago. His eyes narrowed as the freckles on his forehead loosely formed a satanic cross between the lines in his scowl. All of the hatred we'd developed between us was spewing up to the surface and bubbling out of his pores.

"My brother's out cold, and it's all because of you." He stood up, brushed off his overalls and added, "You'd better hope he lives."

The ground shifted under my chest, exposing a mound of soft shale that disintegrated quickly and rattled off the corrugated metal at the bottom of the mineshaft. "I'm losing my grip. Please give me a hand." Billy strolled over to where I was lying and surveyed the damage. I reached up and pleaded, "Give me a hand."

He started to reach down but then hesitated. I could almost see the internal battle going on in his brain over whether to do the right thing or not. It's that same unconscious feeling you get driving down the road where your mind temporarily loses its moral compass and tells you to veer off the road just to see what happens. It's that place, buried in our subconscious, which guides us down a path of either good or evil. Yes, I could tell that Billy had already made up his mind on which way his ethical pendulum was swinging.

With a devious grin he said, "I don't know about a hand, but how about a foot?"

As his foot landed on my hand, I seized it with my other one and yanked as hard as I could. Both his legs left the ground, sending his torso flying down the hill in a tailspin. I could hear him screaming as his body went twirling along the trail like a bobsledder bouncing off stumps and boulders. When he'd made it to the bottom near the creek, his back smacked against a rock so hard that the sound reverberated through the valley. It was loud enough to wake his brother.

Jerry popped up from a muddy pile of leaves onto his hands and surveyed the area. His head rotated back and forth like an animated robot, mindlessly scanning for clues as to what just happened.

"Over here. Help me, Jerry."

He rushed over and grabbed my hand without flinching. Then he pulled as hard as he could, lifting my stomach out of the hole and giving me enough leverage to bring the rest of my body up on my own. He was still searching for his brother as I brushed off the dirt and thanked him.

"Down there," I indicated.

As he scooted down the hillside, I wondered what would've happened had he spotted Billy first. Would he have still pulled me out or would he have left me there to perish in the abyss below? I followed him and reached the creek just as he was lifting his brother's head off the ground.

"Billy, Billy, look at me."

His brother opened his eyes and mumbled, "I can't feel my legs."

Jerry looked up and shouted, "Go get help."

I made eye contact and nodded. Then I shot up the hill as fast as I could. A few steps in, I discovered that my own leg was bleeding so much that the outside of my jeans were soaked in red. I peeked through a rip at my kneecap and saw that there was a deep gash traveling down a few inches.

When I reached the top, I ran over to Hightower's house and started pounding on the back door. Mrs. Hightower opened it. "What's the matter?"

"Billy's hurt down at the bottom of the creek."

Before I could finish my sentence, Mr. Hightower was pushing me out of the doorway and sprinting down the hillside. His wife ran after him. Instead of going back down, I calmly walked over to my house and went to the bathroom. There I opened the medicine cabinet and fumbled around for bandages. My dad was carrying in a box of old papers and taking them to the trash when he noticed the blood spots on the tile floor.

What happened next, I don't quite remember. Everything was a bit hazy after my father sat me down on the sofa and told me to rest. I vaguely recall riding in the car to the hospital and hearing the ambulance carrying Billy pass us by. There were flashes of bright-white ultraviolet lights crossing the ceiling and spinning as they carted me from one room to another. Then there was nothing until I awoke the next morning with a throbbing headache and a swollen, black eye. I gave my statement to Fat Ferny before being discharged, with my father by my side. Thank goodness he was with me because there was enough tension in every stroke of Ferny's pen to string a violin.

Jerry Hightower gave a completely different account of the incident, pinning me as the aggressor. My father insisted on a state policeman being called in due to the conflict of interest between parties. After going over the facts and examining the scene of the accident, the officer interviewed the boy. It didn't take long for him to find one contradiction after another under cross-examination. In the end, Jerry recanted most of his statement and confirmed mine.

Billy never did recover from the blow against the rock. He was paralyzed from the waist down and the future prognosis wasn't good. Over time, there was a chance that his severed spinal cord might gain some motor functions through strenuous rehabilitation, but until then, he was confined to a wheelchair.

Even though it was hard for most people to drum up any kind of sympathy, especially the guys, I couldn't help but feel sorry for him. And perhaps, just a tiny bit guilty. The hardest part was seeing him struggle while getting into their car on mornings when he was scheduled to go to rehab. Both he and his father would glare stonily at my window before pulling out of the driveway.

You know, most people would call this karma. Billy got what he deserved, nothing more, nothing less. A few years ago, I would've accepted that and counted my blessings. But how do you explain what happen to Lonny? How was that karma? After everything that'd happened over the last year, I was beginning to understand why my father was so bitter about losing Mother. There was no karma involved with that tragedy, and if there was a God…well…all I can say is that he was doing a pretty piss poor job lately.

Chapter Fourteen

Business at Nick's Nacks took a turn for the worse after Lonny's funeral. Without him around to entertain everyone, people just didn't stop by like they used to. Joseph and Sally didn't help matters much by moping around all day. Mrs. Blanche tried her best to liven it up by serving cupcakes and coffee with a smile, but things just were never quite the same in that barn. Joseph's health continued to deteriorate, which made it harder for him to help customers load their vehicles. Sometimes, it was so bad that the shop would be closed for days until he felt better.

Sally and I saw each other less and less because she was focused on helping out in the shop, and I was concentrating on making money down out Dukas's. Dad had been spending more time on the road with work. Sometimes he'd call to say that he was too tired to drive home and checking into a hotel. I didn't mind because the guys would usually come over and spend the night. We'd watch TV and eat popcorn until the networks signed off for the evening. I'm glad they did because Hightower had all but secluded himself in the house next door and was beginning to give me the creeps. The State's Attorney had postponed the inquiry into Lonny's death due to the turn of events with the chief's son. On the outside, that seemed like the best thing to do, seeing, that he wasn't in his right mind and all, but, honestly, it just delayed the inevitable. Now everyone was stuck festering in a cloud of uncertainty and assuming the worst.

As the overcast skies replaced the long afternoon shadows and chilly winds stripped most trees of their beauty, people settled in for the long winter. Shutters went up and window screens came out. Swimming pools were drained and leaves were raked into piles to be burned. The scent of hickory drifted from chimneys down into the neighborhoods, lingering long after the smoke had dissipated. Football season came and went with the Buffaloes blowing their chance at winning the Conference on the last game of the season. We did win the Coal Bucket game though. The memories from last year of cracked helmets and dislocated shoulders were still fresh in many of the Wingard players' minds.

Thanksgiving was upon us, and Angie invited me over for dinner. I felt a little guilty about not spending it with my dad and his sister's family, but Angie was pretty insistent on me being there. There was something strange in the way she was acting. She told me which shirt and pants to wear and what not to say about her mother's cooking. It almost felt like she was prepping me to pass some kind of litmus test with her family.

I arrived at the designated time, brushed my shoes off on the mat, and entered into another world. Their house must have been four thousand square feet in size, sitting on five acres of land. It had been designed by an architect from Chicago in the 1960s and included some of the neatest innovations I'd ever seen in a building. The sunlight appeared to follow you from the kitchen to the living room to the bedroom during the day, as if it could anticipate your every move. Even though it was technically three stories high, there were never more than four steps to climb in any one place. But the best feature of the Dukas's castle was the unusual experience with acoustics. Every room was twice the normal size, yet you could hear a pin drop from one corner to the next. But when you went into another room, it was completely void of any sound from the rest of the house.

Mrs. Dukas was barking out orders to her maid and nanny, who doubled as servants on special occasions. Two servants for six guests seemed to be a bit of overkill, but who was I to judge. Dinner started out extremely uneventful, as the conversations never blossomed past your typical everyday small talk and mutual pleasantries. Everyone from Angie's little brother to their annoying grandmother was on their best behavior. After a couple of glasses of chardonnay though, things began to loosen up.

Angie's grandmother started the action. "So, Newbie, I hear that you're an orphan."

"Uh, no ma'am. I live with my father."

"And your mother abandoned you?"

"No, actually, she died in a car wreck."

"I see. Abandonment comes in many shapes and sizes."

"She didn't abandon him, grandmother. She died," interjected Angie.

"Oh honey, you have so much to learn about life."

Mrs. Dukas promptly rolled her eyes and called for dessert to be served. She tried to change the subject before her mother could begin another sentence. "It's so very sad to hear about Tony Hightower's boy. That must have been tragic."

I didn't know how to respond. Angie was squeezing my knee under the table, no doubt, signaling me to be as polite as possible. "Uh, yes it was."

"Yes, indeed. Between Billy Hightower's injury, and Bobby McIntosh and Lonny Nack dying, there's been quite a lot of bad news in Bunsen Creek. I think it's a sign that we are approaching the end of time."

"Now Virginia, a couple of deaths in a small town isn't a sign that it's the end of time." Alistair plopped another serving of mashed potatoes on his plate. "In fact, I never liked any of those boys."

"Lonny was one heck of a harmonica player though," chimed in Angie's little brother.

Angie squeezed my knee again and said, "I don't think any of us should be talking about the dead like this. It's not…proper."

"Scumbags every one of them," gargled out their grandmother.

And with that, I excused myself to the restroom. Angie came after me a few minutes later, knowing why I'd left. She stood in front of the bathroom door and said, "Newbie, I'm sorry about my family. Don't let them get to you. They don't mean any harm. They just don't know any better." She paused for a moment and then added, "Besides, I don't plan on living in this place forever. In fact, as soon as I graduate, I'm moving into our rental house out on the west end of town. Maybe you can move in too."

What a grand thought that was. I could see the two of us living there, both working in the shop, hosting barbeques, lying around the swimming pool, and raising kids. What a grand thought, indeed.

Mr. Dukas appeared behind Angie and said, "Ah, there you are. Where's Newbie?"

"He's still in the bathroom."

I could tell that it was time to rejoin the party, so I opened the door. "I'm right here, sir."

"Wonderful. How would you like to join me in my study?"

"Of course."

I'd never been in a room that was actually called a "study" before, so this was quite a treat. Come to find out, it was nothing more than his office with a few books. I scanned the shelves and quickly realized that besides a couple of sets of encyclopedias, he had a sparse collection of mismatched classic novels, no doubt purchased at rummage sales, and a few college textbooks.

"Newbie, I'd offer you a drink but that would be inappropriate. Would you like a cigar?"

"I'd rather have that drink, sir."

"So be it. Just as long as the women don't find out. Scotch or bourbon?"

I, of course, didn't have a clue to what the difference was between them so I said the first thing that came to mind. "Bourbon on the rocks."

As Mr. Dukas was pouring our drinks, he said, "Sorry about the comments back there at the dinner table. Mother can be…how do I put it…a complete bitch."

"That's quite alright."

"Still, it was rude, and I should have not said what I said about those boys."

"Apology accepted."

He stirred the drinks and handed me my glass. I felt like Cary Grant in the movie *North By Northwest,* right before they drugged him and staged the accident. It's that moment between anticipation and recognition, where anything can happen that could change your life forever.

"You know, my son shows no interest in working at the store. I've tried repeatedly to spark his curiosity but…he just doesn't seem to care. That means there's an opening for someone to take over the reign when I retire…and I plan to retire real soon."

"I'm not sure what you're saying, sir."

"What I'm saying, Newbie, is that I like you a lot. Angie likes you a lot. And if you play your cards right, there might just be a future here taking over the family business."

After hearing this last comment, the glass almost slipped out of my hand. The only thing left to do was down the whole drink. I nearly gagged as my throat burned and quietly coughed up what was left of my youth. Here I was negotiating my future and a hand in marriage without ever having to say a word. I wondered, *Is this how things are done in the real world?*

He could sense that his last statement was a bit overwhelming. "You know, I grew up in a pretty rough neighborhood in New York. If you wanted to get ahead, you had to fight for it. And even then, you could end up in the gutter. But what I'm offering you is a chance of a lifetime."

I nodded. "I know, but what makes you think that Angie's just going to go along with this?"

"Leave Angie to me, son."

A knock came from outside as Angie slid open the French doors. "Daddy, what are you two up to in here?"

I could only assume that her comment was sincere, but a part of me wondered if she was in on the whole thing.

"Nothing, my dear. He's all yours."

And with that, Angie escorted me to the living room where we played board games for the next few hours. As the gray skies dimmed and darkness set in, we made our way to the side of the house and eventually into the garage. It must have been all of thirty degrees in there, but Angie just placed her finger over my lips. "Follow me."

When we reached the far corner, she pulled out a ladder and climbed to the top. Carefully, she lifted the ceiling tile and retrieved a key. I helped her down as she whispered, "Be quiet. My dad doesn't know I know."

"Know what?"

"You'll see."

Behind a curtain and mounted against the back wall was a large wooden case about a foot deep and four feet square. She had to slide a few boxes out of the way in order to get to the padlock. She removed it and opened the doors into her father's deepest darkest secret. Inside was a set of wide-bladed steel knives, at least twelve inches long, with metal handles that were painted red or white. They were attached to a metal plate that was obviously magnetic and fanned out like turkey feathers in a half circle. Behind them was what first appeared to be a dartboard, but after closer observation, I realized that it didn't have any numbers on it. Instead, it was divided into eight separate sections with a bullseye in the middle and a set of human skulls around the perimeter.

"Whoa…what the heck is this?"

"It's a knife throwing set. My dad is obsessed with it. He comes out here a few times a week and practices. I mean look at that board."

Sure enough, the corked board had more gashes and pockets than the moon's surface. In the corner of the case, was a plastic folder with targets inside. I lifted one out and unfolded it. It was the silhouette of a life-size human body.

"What's he do with these?" I asked.

"He keeps the door locked when he practices, but I'm pretty sure he tacks the posters to the wall over here and throws at them." Next to the case was a sheet of plywood nailed to the wall. The middle of the board was smooth and unblemished but the outline of a person's body could easily be seen in the marks around the edges.

"This is so cool. Have you ever asked him about it?"

"No, I'm not sure I want to know."

There was a voice calling from inside the house. Angie quickly closed the case and secured the padlock. Then she climbed the ladder and returned the key to its hiding place. We ducked out the side door and entered the house from the back yard.

Soon after Thanksgiving, the first snow fell and, with that, came the answer to all of our prayers. Call it serendipity or just plain dumb luck, but either way, our wishes were finally answered. The story was told to us second-hand by Rudy, our self-designated gossipmonger of local news traveling around the tavern circuit. It seems that the Colonel had been drinking down at Hank's Oasis all evening, celebrating Lonny's twenty-first birthday. After a half dozen shots, eight beers, and two or three eulogies, he was barely able to sit on a bar stool. He was off on another tirade about Jesus and self-cleaning car washes when, all of a sudden, he started crying. Now, mind you, I wasn't there, but according to Rudy, he kept mumbling, "That Hightower bastard," repeatedly under his breath. Then he started getting louder and louder.

I should probably stop here and back up a step to fill you in on another situation going on simultaneously. The State's Attorney had unexpectedly died in a skiing accident a few weeks earlier. Since there were only a few months left in his term, the Board of Supervisors appointed his assistant to replace him. On paper, it made perfect sense as the state would be saving money by not having a special election and the charter bylaws did spell out that it was at their discretion to handle the matter however they saw fit. Little did they know that, Bernard Bates, a.k.a. Bardy, the newly appointed State's Attorney, was a certified alcoholic, as I'd mentioned earlier.

Bardy left work every night around five o'clock, went to his Dodge van and changed into another outfit before heading off for the evening. He'd even adopted a completely new identity depending on which night of the week it was. On Mondays, he was a sailor named Pete who'd served in Vietnam and earned the Purple Heart. On Tuesdays, he was a Maytag repairman named Bud, and so on. Tonight he was Arnie the mailman and having a merry old time drinking in Hank's Oasis. He was minding his own business and enjoying this chubby preacher in a white cowboy hat ramble on about losing his best friend. If nothing else, Colonel Remus P. Entwhistle was entertaining.

"Go on, Rudy, finish the story," I said.

"Do you guys have any beer left?"

We all looked at him with disbelief. "You're our beer guy, Bozo. If you didn't bring it, then we don't have it."

"Oh yeah," he replied. "Anyway, the Colonel broke down crying and started mumbling something about a pig flying through the air. He kept saying, 'My, oh my, how that pig did fly,' over and over again like it was some kind of nursery rhyme, while swinging his arm back and forth in the air. Then he went quiet for minute and shouted, 'That freaking murderer,' at the top of his lungs. This mailman sitting at the end of the bar came up to him and asked what he was talking about. The Colonel spilled his guts and went on about how Lonny was alive when he left that night of the accident, and when the ambulance arrived, he was dead. The only person around in between that time was Hightower. Then he went on to tell him how Hightower had threatened Lonny after the streaking incident, saying that he would make him pay for embarrassing him in front of the whole town. I barely heard what he was saying from where I was sitting, but I heard enough. Turns out that this mailman is really the new State's Attorney. I mean, he didn't quite come out and say it, but the bartender confirmed it after he left. There was a business card lying on the floor under his seat."

"Holy Mary Mother of Jesus," exclaimed Buzzard.

"Rudy, this calls for a celebration," said Skeeter. "Here's a five spot. Will you go pick us up a six pack?"

"I'll pick you up two six packs," and with that, Rudy disappeared and never returned. It didn't matter though. We were so hyped up on adrenaline that the natural high was more than enough.

The next day, there were a dozen cars in and out of Hightower's driveway; the mayor was there, city council members, the state police, you name it. Neither Hightower nor his wife came out of the house, not even to pick up the mail. I looked in the paper every night for any news about Lonny's death, but there was nothing. It was obvious that they were keeping the story hush-hush for some reason. I suspected that the Colonel had gotten cold feet and recanted everything when he was sober. There was also the possibility that Bardy Bates had to tread lightly in explaining how he'd come about this information. Plus, there was the fact that this was all speculation and circumstantial. None of it would hold up in a court of law.

For a few days, we didn't know how this was going to turn out. Then, much like that unexpected Christmas present buried underneath the tree you find after all of the wrappers are picked up, it happened. It was Christmas Eve and everybody in town had gone home for the evening to be with their families except for one: that friendly realtor from RE/MAX who pulled in front of Hightower's house and planted a "For Sale" sign in his front lawn. I called the boys and told them that this was going to be the best Christmas ever. We watched *A Christmas Carol* on TV and ate homemade waffle cookies that Skeeter's mom had baked throughout the evening.

"God bless everyone," I kept saying after every bite.

The loading van backed up to the house during Spring Break and began moving the Hightower's furniture to its new destination. Rumor was that he had sold the house to Alistair Dukas and was moving over to Indiana. There wasn't enough evidence to convict him of murder, but the State's Attorney office did find in their report that he was negligent in his duties and had unnecessarily endangered the public by pursuing a pig robber in a high-speed chase, resulting in the death of an innocent youth. He was forced to resign his post as Chief of Police. In order to survive, he sold the house, downsized, and went looking for another job. Peabody Mines hired him within weeks as a security guard to watch over their operations. It was definitely a step down, but the salary paid the bills.

The boys and I sat in my driveway on lawn chairs and wallowed in our glory as the Hightowers barked orders to the movers. Billy Hightower rolled back and forth from the garage to the street, trying to act busy with an item or two sitting on his lap. His father glared over every once in a while. Each time, it was directed straight at me. Even the other guys took notice and stopped gloating. I could only imagine what was going on in his mind. No doubt, he still blamed me for his son's injuries and was festering all kinds of hostilities deep inside.

I invited Sally over to join in the festivities, hoping that it would cheer her up, but she was not in the celebratory mood. Her father had suffered a mild stroke and wasn't able to work. The store had been closed for a month, and the rumor was that all of the items had been sold to Junkie Joe's over in Indiana. Revenge can be sweet, but sometimes no amount of reparation can ever heal the soul.

I debated whether to tell her everything about Bardy Bates and Hightower. The only thing stated in the newspapers was about how he had endangered the public and was indirectly responsible for the death of Bobby McIntosh. Part of the plea bargain was that no charges would be filed against him. I figured that telling her about how he might have murdered Lonny would just cause more damage than good. Plus, now with the news of her father's poor health, a story like that might just push him passed the point of no return. She was so distant those days anyway. Most of our conversations never went more than a few words, as her mind seemed to be elsewhere.

Alistair Dukas was enjoying a banner year at the discount store. Business was up so much that he hired another sales clerk to handle the extra volume. A neon light had been installed out front of the shop on the square, and store hours were extended to nine o'clock. Angie had even begun working a few nights a week when needed. This, of course, meant that we saw more and more of each other. I must admit, working there with her in the store for the rest of my life didn't seem like such a bad idea.

After Hightower left town, things settled down, and everything went back to normal. Most of us were over the thrill of high school traditions like making freshman carry our books and calling us "Mister" in the hallways. The senior girls finally started noticing us again, but by then, we were so tainted by the way they'd treated us the last three years that the thought of dating them was not even attractive. That didn't stop us from hooking up occasionally. I mean, in a couple of months, everybody would be going their own separate ways, and the opportunity might never come again.

Skeeter's job at GM after graduation was a done deal, and T.J. had secured a job in the coal mines. I still had to decide between the store, the mines, or college. Buzzard had already accepted a place at the U of I, but I was still in limbo.

"Dude, just accept the offer. You don't have to pay anything more until the fall."

"You're right. What can it hurt?" Buzzard was right, but the door on the coal mining job was closing fast. Yet, somehow, I think it had already shut. Who in their right mind would choose a job working hundreds of feet underground in the dark cold ground over lying in bed next to one of the prettiest girls in town?

Still, there was one little problem that I'd been avoiding way too long but couldn't any longer: talking to my dad about college. I don't think either one of us wanted to face this issue head on because it meant closure, and we'd both have to deal with the fact that I was all grown up. Then there was the harsh reality of figuring out how to pay for it. When he came through the door that evening and saw me sitting at the kitchen table, we both knew the time had come.

"Newbie, we need to talk." He grabbed the acceptance letter from the counter and fumbled around with it as he continued, "Quite an achievement here."

"Dad, I don't need to go there. I can still work at Dukas's and go to junior college instead."

"I wish I had the money to send you, son, but I don't. We can try student loans and see how much they'll give us, and I'll do whatever else I can to help out with the rest. Maybe I can take out a loan on the house." He half smiled as a tear formed in his eye. Then he looked away.

"Don't worry, Pop. It's not that big a deal."

"Oh, but it is. Your mom would turn over in her grave if you didn't go."

"We'll figure something out. Besides, I just can't leave you here all alone. I mean, who's gonna take care of you?"

Then he lowered his head and was quiet for a moment. Without looking up he said, "Son, I need to tell you something else. I've met another woman."

"Wha…How…" was all I could get out of my mouth.

"Yes, it's getting kind of serious, too. So I thought you should know as we'll be hanging out more together."

"How did this happen? And do I know her?"

"I think so. She's one of your teachers at school. Her name is Mya Lenhart."

Not only did my world blow apart that night, it was also reborn. A cloak of uncertainty had been lifted. I no longer had a sentient feeling of obligation and commitment hanging over my life. I felt free. "You mean Miss Glandhard? That is so cool, Pop," was all I could think to say. "That is so cool."

My dad just grinned, shook his head, and whispered, "Miss Glandhard, of course."

That last week of school, the boys and I decided that it was time to test the waters at Hank's Oasis to see if we could get served. After all, we'd been paying customers of the place for years, just never sitting at the actual bar. Skeeter had secured a few fake driver's licenses from his older brother who didn't need them anymore. So, on a Tuesday night, with an almost empty bar, we walked in through the back door, bellied up to four bar seats like we'd done it a hundred times before, and sat down.

Hank was at the front of the bar, sitting in a chair and talking to a regular customer. He peered down at us, finished his cigarette in an ashtray, and made the long, slow trek over to where we were sitting. He'd been in a car accident years earlier which left him favoring his right leg and a little hard of hearing out one of his ears. He placed a bowl of peanuts on the bar, turned his head to the side, and asked, "What'll it be, boys?"

"Budweiser, on tap," said Skeeter with gusto.

"You have an I.D.?"

Skeeter pulled it out and showed it to Hank. He studied the fake driver's license and then glanced at his face. He matched up the brown hair, brown eyes and estimated Skeeter's weight. They all seemed to match. Thank God, there was no photo on the card. I couldn't help but think that Skeeter had planned for this day since he was a little kid, knowing that if we all had nicknames, no one would know our real names. Right then, all we could hope was that Hank was one of them.

Hank handed it back and turned to Buzzard, "Where's yours?" Buzzard pulled his fake I.D. out while Skeeter slipped his behind his back to T.J. sitting on the other end.

"Okay, where's yours?" he asked me. I leaned back into the shadows and gave him the one with an out of town address. I just crossed my fingers and prayed that he hadn't seen me walking around town lately and didn't know who I was. To our delight, Hank looked bored with the whole ritual and just glanced at the last two.

"Four Budweisers it is."

"Uh, could you make mine a Busch?" asked Buzzard. I almost yanked him out of his seat and dragged him into the bathroom to ask what the freaking bejesus he was doing, but the saner side of me prevailed.

"Three Buds and a Busch it is."

We'd done it. We tipped him more than the price of the beers, and it was home free for the rest of the night.

"To your mother," I said.

"To your mother," they all chimed.

"To Lonny Nack." There was a moment of silence after that proposed toast. We just clanked our glasses together, smiled, and downed our beers; enough said.

We drank the first two within five minutes and were feeling a good buzz. So good that I dug out a quarter and decided to play the jukebox. In honor of my mother and the fact that we'd succeeded in making it to that next level of manhood, I played D9, "Ring of Fire" by Johnny Cash. It was her favorite. As the alcohol made its way down to my beat-stomping foot while it crunched a floor full of peanut shells, I tried to absorb the whole scene and reflect on our accomplishment. Life was good. Of course, we all knew that Lonny had started drinking at Hank's when he was only fifteen. Something about a muscular boy with a tattoo and a Mohawk haircut led you to the conclusion that he deserved a drink, no matter what the age.

T.J. and Buzzard put a quarter in the pool table and racked them up. T.J. was an excellent shot but Buzzard was luckier than all get out. I pulled out a five spot, ordered another round and went to the restroom in the back. The toilet was the only stall working as someone had decided to take out his frustrations on the urinal. I shook my head in disgust over the injustice thrust upon this innocent piece of porcelain until I looked up and read the graffiti above it, "Don't chew the Trojan gum, it tastes like rubber."

On my way out, I noticed someone sitting in the shadows of the corner booth. His hat looked familiar. I stopped to zip up my pants and heard, "Hello, Newbie." I stared for a minute, trying to focus in the dark, but it wasn't until he finally angled his head into the direction of the overhead pool table light that I realized it was Dante. He motioned me over. "Have a seat."

"Why Danny, how've you been?"

"Oh, I'm doin' just about right. How about you boys? Out celebrating something?"

"Just out having a beer."

He nodded and leaned in, "I heard you toasting Lonny Nack there earlier. Tragic accident, wasn't it?"

"It sure was. He died way before his time." I was still, at least, two more drinks away from telling him what I really thought about Lonny's death, but that didn't stop me from whispering under my breath, "Accident my ass."

Dante quickly looked up with his left eye cocked, straining to hear what I'd said and waiting for more. Instead, I tried to change the subject. "How's the fishing down at the dam?"

"Off and on." He tapped on his beer glass for a few bars of "I Walk the Line" before adding, "Hear we have a new police chief. What do you think of Ferny?"

"Much better than the last one. That's for sure."

"I heard they ran him out of town…poor guy."

My jaw dropped, almost in rhythm with the jukebox needle as the third and last song I'd played began. "Poor guy, he was a…I mean, the man was the worst. If you only knew."

"Knew what, about Lonny Nack's murder?" The scar on his neck glistened off the pool light as he lifted his glass and took a drink. Then he placed the mug on the table and chuckle-burped as Johnny sang the first verse on the jukebox. I couldn't tell whether his sneer was sincere or cynical. A man with a reputation like his was hard to read.

"You think he was murdered?" I questioned.

Dante chuckle-burped again, raised his glass high into the air, and shouted in between verses, "Hank, two more beers." Then he stared me down and sputtered, "You betcha, but you already knew that now didn't you?"

I just nodded as he wiped the spit from his lip.

"Problem is, sonny, the wrong person took the rap."

"What do you mean?" I exclaimed. Now I was spitting up syllables.

He grinned and shook his head back and forth. "Hightower didn't do it. I was there." In that moment, I had a vision of Dante standing at the river's edge with a fishing pole wedged into the sand. Simultaneously, I saw Lonny's truck trying to make the turn at the dam and rolling out of control. Hank arrived with two beers and Dante slipped him a bill. "Thank ye."

"You were there." It wasn't a question; it was an epiphany.

"Yep, I heard the crash. I was ready to run up the hill when my line started bobbing, I mean, not bobbing like a little bit, but bouncing up and down. I caught the pole just before it disappeared into the water. Let me tell you, it was the biggest darn catfish I'd ever seen, and I wasn't about to let it get away and take my pole with it. I chased it downstream about twenty feet and then back again. I brung him up though. It was a battle, but I brung him up. When it came out of the water, the damn line snapped in two. As you can imagine, I almost shit my britches seeing that fish squirming back into the water. So I reached out and caught that sucker, yes by golly, I caught him right before he went under." He lifted his hand and pointed at a scar between his thumb and pointer finger, "Damn fish tore into me something terrible. Well, I tossed the bastard onto the shore and hit it over the head with a rock. Then I ran up the hill."

He took a swig of his beer and continued, "When I got to the top, I heard some yelling and a loud splash. There was Hightower's car in the parking lot, so I ran up and looked inside. Hightower was still in his seat belt moaning. He looked a little dinged up, but I could tell he'd be fine. Then I saw Lonny's truck. It was sinking into the water, sonny." He shook his head and took another drink. "Whew, it didn't look good. By the time I got over there, it was too late. The truck was long gone, and there was no way I could pull it out."

He chugged the rest of the beer and waved it in the air toward Hank. Dante plopped his mug on the table and said, "All I can tell you is that when I was running over to Lonny's truck, Alistair Dukas was walking away back to his house."

"Mr. Dukas?" My mind was spinning in a figure eight, trying hard to comprehend what he'd just said. I looped in the Colonel's account and recalled what I'd witnessed at the scene. Everything Dante had said seemed to fit into place. Trying hard to make sense of it all, I asked, "Where was Colonel Entwhistle?"

Dante shook his head. "Never saw him. Must've gone for help by then, I guess."

I took a sip, rewound all of the details again, and played them back. Something was missing. Then it hit me. "Why didn't you tell the police?"

"Who, Hightower? Who was he gonna believe, me or the richest man in town? After all, he and Lonny weren't quite the best of friends, you know." He laughed and slapped his hand on his knee. "Boy, you gotta lotta growing up to do."

He was right. When it comes to truth, it's not the content that makes it believable as much as the deliverer of the message. Somewhere in our history, society had elevated the word of a successful businessman above that of a poor old fisherman, no matter how unscrupulous he might be. Money somehow had become synonymous with prestige, which unfortunately had become synonymous with honesty. Of course, anyone who'd been on the wrong end of a business deal could tell you how far from the truth that was. At that moment, all I could think about was poor Joseph Nack.

Hank brought over the beer and asked if I needed anything else. "A shot of whiskey. Make it a double." As he walked away, I said, "Danny, it's been nice talking to you. I hope the fish keep biting."

Back at the bar, my drink arrived, and I chugged it before anyone had the chance to say, "To your mother."

Buzzard and T.J. were still shooting pool, but Skeeter turned around just in time to watch the glass hit the bar. "What the…"

I just shook my head as the whiskey numbed every nerve in my body. "Don't ask."

"Don't ask? Jesus, Newbie, you're talking more like a girl every minute. What do you mean don't ask?" He looked to the back door where Dante hid in the shadows and added, "And when did you and Dante become buddies?"

"We're fishing buddies. I ran into him one morning when we were camping down at the cove. His actual name is Danny. He goes there and fishes all the time."

"Yeah, well what did you two talk about?"

For some reason, I didn't know how to begin the next sentence. How do you start a sentence with, "My girlfriend's father…" or, "My boss…" or, "The biggest freaking person in town…" and end it with, "Is a murderer"? Finally, I just said, "Not much…fishing and stuff."

"Fishing…and now you're doing shots?"

"Yep. Why not?"

Skeeter peered over the pool table to the back of the bar, but it was empty. Dante had left. "That old man is crazy, you know."

"Maybe, but he's not half as bad as people make him out to be."

"Probably not."

I ran my finger over the rim of my glass for a minute and said, "You know, what if Hightower didn't do it?"

"Do what?"

"Kill Lonny. I mean, there's really no evidence that he did, and now he's…you know, been run out of town. I can't help but feel a little guilty about it, considering what we tried to do and all."

Skeeter grabbed my arm. "Newbie, Tony Hightower was a prick… with a capital P. He put the 'ick' in the word 'prick.' When you look up 'dickhead' in the dictionary, there's a picture of Hightower. Do you get where I'm going with this? I feel more guilty about not sending you a thank you card for buying me a beer than I do about sending that prick-face-anal-muncher on his merry way."

I chuckled. "You always did have a way with words."

We returned to the Backroom that night, successfully breaking the bar stool barrier. For some reason, I just couldn't tell them about what Dante had said. I don't know if it was because I didn't believe it myself, or I was still in shock. Either way, there was so much more at stake now, and I had to figure out what to do next. Telling the police wasn't going to really do any good. Fat Ferny had no more love for Lonny than Hightower did. Confronting Mr. Dukas might work to my advantage as I could hold it over his head. On the other hand, it might get me killed. Eventually, I dozed off dreaming about fishing, college, girlfriends; you name it. They were all there in Technicolor, flashing across my eyelids.

Graduation was upon us and with that came the inevitable set of drawn-out goodbyes to our classmates. We kissed the girls, hugged the guys, and ended up one last time at Skeeter's to celebrate. We all sat on the front porch, watched the traffic coming up and down West Street and made a pact to never lose touch with each other.

"What are you going to do with your graduation money?"

"I think I'll go to Chicago next weekend and see a ball game," said T.J.

"I think I'll buy a new camera. Maybe take some nude photos of Mary Makowski and send them to Newbie," kidded Skeeter.

"I think I'll look up that cheerleader from Wingard who gave me her phone number a few months ago. Maybe take her out and show her a good time," added Buzzard.

I didn't say a word. My mind had drifted off miles away and hardly heard anything they'd said. All three of them stared at me until Skeeter chimed in, "Hey, Newbie. What's up with the silent treatment?"

"Sorry, I was just thinking about something."

"Well what, for God's sake?" asked Buzzard.

"It's nothing," I answered.

"You're not getting off that easy. What's up?"

I looked to each one of them and sighed. Even though we were best friends and all, opening up and confiding your deepest dark secrets was still uncomfortable. My mind was swirling with questions and scenarios about what could happen if I revealed what Dante had told me. I'd be throwing away a lifetime on Easy Street by revealing everything now.

"I don't know. I'm still undecided on what I want to do. I mean, Mr. Dukas offered to promote me in the store, there's the job in the mines, and then there's college. Right now, I just can't make up my mind."

T.J. strolled up in front of me and stared straight into my eyes. Then he leaned in and said, "Newbie, you know some people are born lucky. I mean you don't get to pick your parents, how rich you are, or the color of your skin. There are other kinds of luck too though. I'm talking about those times in your life when opportunity knocks and tells you to shit or get off the pot. That's what's happening to you right now. I know you think everything is so screwed up and are feeling a little bit sorry for yourself, but you shouldn't. Most people would kill to be in your place right now."

"I guess you're right."

"Of course, I'm right, pencil-dick."

Skeeter walked up in between us, patted us both on the back, and said, "Simmer down, you two. You know what we need? We need to have one last hurrah. One big-ass, week-long, celebration where we can let it all hang out. I know what we should do with our money. How about a road trip to Daytona Beach?"

And with that, we packed up Buzzard's Dodge Charger with extra clothes, swimming trunks, sunglasses, food, water, and everything else we'd need to lay on the sand for a few days and watch the bikinis walk by. Yes, it was going to be one whole week full of drinking, swimming, eating, drinking some more…and maybe lovemaking. When Skeeter tossed his suitcase in the trunk and plopped a sack full of condoms on the front seat, I knew we were in for a good time. Thirteen hours into the drive, I was beginning to have my doubts.

Somewhere on a highway running through Georgia, the clutch went out in Buzzard's Dodge, and we were stuck at a back roads gas station for three hours. Every time a truck would drive by and slow down with two good ole boys in it and a shotgun hanging in the rear window, a banjo plucked out the opening lines of *Deliverance* in the back of my mind. We had to use every last dollar between us to pay the bill before the station attendant would let us leave. Thankfully, Gus came through and wired us money when we arrived in Daytona.

Our luck changed once we hit the beach and the partying commenced. We were back in good spirits, mentally and physically, but what I can remember about the next few days is now very sketchy. We didn't need fake I.D.s in Florida, as the drinking age was eighteen. That one factor must have guided ten thousand other teenagers to Daytona that week because you couldn't help but trip over a passed-out drunk every five minutes or walk into a room with a keg. When T.J. pulled out a wad of dollar bills and said, "Strip club?" I knew we were in for a long night.

Now the closest we'd ever gotten to a naked woman dancing around a pole was whatever Hugh Hefner provided between the pages of those worn-out magazines in Skeeter's Backroom. Seeing it live and in the flesh was not only erotic, it was also a bit eerie. In fact, I'd go as far to say it got down right creepy. We weren't prepared for drooping breasts being pressed against our shoulders and faces. No matter how many dollar bills we tossed at the situation or how much alcohol we tried to calm our nerves with, there was still an awkward uneasiness making us squirm in our seats every time a lady came over to introduce herself.

A funny thing happened as soon as we walked out of the club though. On the way back to the hotel, our recollection of the evening's events began to change almost immediately. All of a sudden, Buzzard's face didn't turn white when the girl licked the side of his cheek. It turned red and hot. The gal that kept placing my hand on her rear as she sat on my lap was now being spanked, according to Skeeter. T.J., who'd spent most of the night running back and forth to the restroom, but was now being escorted by a beautiful woman every time. The farther away we walked from the scene, the further from the truth the stories became. By the time we exited the hotel elevator and made our way to the next floor party, our night's prowess had been broadcast to anyone and everyone who'd listen.

It was only natural for the rest of the evening to continue in the same vein. We'd gained a whole new sense of machismo that couldn't be contained.

Buzzard decided that he didn't need his glasses any longer and spent the rest of the night running into walls while trying to look cool. The hotel was in the process of building an addition near our rooms, and someone had taken down the barricade between structures. Skeeter and I had climbed out the window and were mingling in with some other partygoers at the construction site. We were looking down at the pool below while entertaining a couple of older sorority sisters with little white lies about just finishing our first year at the U of I when Buzzard walked up.

What happened after that went something like this:

"Hey Buzzard, come meet Donna and Dana. They're from the University of Alabama."

"Alabama. Isn't that Bear Bryant's school?"

"You betcha. The Crimson Tide, ya'll," added Dana with a sweet southern drawl.

"Don't you just love that accent, Buzzard?" crooned Skeeter as he winked and smiled.

"Speaking of tide, I could do with a little swim tonight. Any one up for skinny dipping?"

About that time, Buzzard walked over to what he thought was the nozzle to a keg only to find himself unchaining the rope separating him from the edge of the roof. The next thing we know, he's falling two stories down directly onto and then through a canvass awning by the deep end of the pool. The girls screamed so loud that someone heard them over the booming stereo in the other room and turned it off.

"Oh my God, he just jumped off the roof."

"We need to go see if he's alright."

Everyone shuffled down the stairway as fast as they could and raced over to the poolside. When we got there, two guys were smoking a joint and sitting in patio chairs next to the awning. Without the slightest inclination that something terribly wrong had just happened, one of them said, "Hey, this dude just fell out of the sky."

The other guy then said, "Ask him if he wants a hit."

In another place and time, I would have laughed until I cried, but not tonight. I turned to Buzzard who was moaning and rubbing his ankle. The two girls rushed to his side and asked, "Are you alright?"

He couldn't even look them in the eye. He just put his head down and replied, "I think so. My knees scuffed up and my ankle hurts, but I'll survive."

Skeeter immediately recognized the predicament Buzzard, and the rest of us by default, were now in as a direct result of his visual miscalculation. Not only would there be the constant ribbing from everyone and their brother for the next few days, we'd surely lose all of the gains we'd made with the two girls. The wheels started churning in that emphatic brain of his and within seconds, he knew what to say.

"Well, the next time you want to go skinny dipping, stud, first you need to take off all your clothes, then you need to get the girls to take off their clothes, and, most of all, you need to get a better running jump at the pool."

Buzzard's reply was spot on. "I was trying to take my clothes off in mid-air."

The girls giggled, and the ruse was complete. Instead of an embarrassing funny anecdote circulating around about a guy accidentally falling out of a window and nearly killing himself, we had a swaggering tale about the guy who tried to jump into the pool from the second story. Buzzard spent the next two days lying on a lawn chair near poolside being nursed back to health by the two sisters.

Men would stroll by every few minutes and shout, "Right on, brother."

Women would walk up and place a soft kiss on his forehead and whisper, "You're a wild man." Behind a pair of prescription sunglasses and a bandaged leg, he was the King of Spades for the rest of the week. We all soaked up the sun and bask in his glory while sipping funny colored drinks with umbrellas until the sun went down.

If I had it my way, I'd still be sitting next to that pool today. Packing up our bags was a bittersweet ending to one kick-ass week, but funds were running low, and we knew it was best to leave on a high note. When we tossed our suitcases in the car, Skeeter's bag of condoms fell out and landed onto the ground. T.J. picked it up, looked inside and asked, "How many rubbers did you bring?"

"A dozen."

T.J. tossed the bag into the trunk and said, "I count thirteen."

That didn't bring us down though. As we pulled away and exited the hotel parking lot, people wished us well and waved goodbye. Girls were yelling from the windows, "See ya, wild man." I couldn't help but laugh inside about how we had serendipitously taken such a potentially horrible situation and made it into something wonderful.

We'd created enjoyment out of unjoyment. Hey, I just made up another word.

On the drive back to Illinois, we couldn't stop talking about the adventures we'd had, whether they were real or not. It made the drive go so quickly. Skeeter's plan to make me forget about the choices I needed to face in the coming months had worked. Unfortunately, I was no closer to figuring out what I was going to do. Yet, a lot had been accomplished on this trip. We'd crossed over that line into manhood, and any remnants of the awkward teenagers that began the trip had vanished. Not only did we abandon any inhibitions about who we were or what we could be, we'd discovered that the key to raising hell wasn't so much about the deed itself as it was in the way you conveyed it to the world. The trick was to not worry so much about the facts, but just make sure the myth was intact. With that thought in mind, it was no surprise to find out after we arrived home and unloaded the car, that the bag of condoms had vanished too.

Chapter Fifteen

A few days after our trip, I walked down to Bunsen Creek to think things out. It was the one place where I felt completely free from all of my troubles and alone with myself. The serenity and emerald beauty that blanketed those hills always calmed my nerves. Hopefully, today it would help me find my way.

Many of the trees on the other side of the stream had been chopped down and carted away leaving gaping holes for the sunlight to shine down to the surface. A light rain had blown in that morning, cleansing everything of any residue from the night before. The birds were in full chorus, coaxing the sun to come out with song and filling the valley like a symphony.

There were no signs of Mother's voice drifting through the air today. In fact, her image was harder and harder for me to see in my mind, let alone through the trees. I closed my eyes and concentrated. "Are you there, Mom?" I whispered. "If so, please come back and talk for a while. I really need you now." I sat for the longest time, but nothing happened. Finally, I got up and walked to the top of the hill on the other side.

Old Man Tranchant's place stood there like a tombstone, dark, cold, and abandoned. The grass was knee-high and his riding lawnmower was still sitting in the same spot it was before he died. I couldn't help but think of how the town had changed since his death and the fire. That block of the square still sat barren and forgotten.

From the other side of the hill, came a voice. "Newbie, are you there?"

It was my father waving a newspaper from my backyard.

"Over here, Dad."

He spotted me but didn't move. I could sense that something was keeping him from walking down the hill. Maybe he had his own demons to contend with in that valley.

"I'm coming," I yelled.

When I reached our backyard, he greeted me with a smile. "Newbie, come here and look at this."

He unfolded the newspaper and showed me the headlines, "New Lake for Bunsen Creek."

I grabbed it and scanned the article as he filled me in. "They're building a lake right here in our backyard. The Governor just signed the bill authorizing funds."

"How did this happen? I mean, why didn't we know about this sooner?"

"It says that a private firm is paying for most of it. A company called The Allistania Corporation out of Chicago. I guess that's why it wasn't public knowledge." Then he placed both his hands on my shoulders. "Do you know what this means? It means that they'll be buying our land down in the valley. And that means we'll have money for college."

I tried my best to look happy, but something else was racing through my mind and preventing me from enjoying the moment. I knew that name. I'd seen it a dozen times on boxes and envelopes in Dukas's dumpster. Maybe Lonny had seen it too. All of a sudden, my eyes were seeing Bunsen Creek Valley in a different light.

"This calls for a celebration. I'll call Mya, and let's go out to dinner."

"That sounds great and all, but I have to go into work today."

"Okay then, we'll go out tomorrow night. And we'll talk about the boat dock we're going to build once the lake is done. Can you imagine, a lake in our back yard? I can almost see it now." He looked a bit giddy standing there and thinking about all of the possibilities. It was a side of him I hadn't seen in years. I don't think it had even registered to him that the place where they would be filling the valley up with water was where he and Mother had met. On the other hand, maybe he was now over that part of his life and ready to move on.

I had the late shift, which, at the end of the month, meant closing the store and doing inventory. It would just be Alistair and me for two whole hours. My mind was miles away that evening as I swept the floors, set up displays and attended to customers. Alistair spent most of the night in his office with the door closed. I went over the scenario a hundred times trying to think of what to say, if anything.

When it was closing time, he came out of his office and locked the front door. Then he pulled a bulletin board off the wall and said, "Newbie, are you ready to start the inventory?"

I came out of the storage room with a box cutter and a pair of scissors in my pockets. They weren't the best weapons, but I wanted to be ready just in case this thing went south. "Yeah, I'm ready, but I need to ask you a question first."

"Well, spit it out."

"What's the Allistania Corporation?"

He took a step back and sized me up. I could tell that the comment troubled him. "You read the paper today, I take it."

I nodded.

"What do you think it is?"

"Mr. Dukas, I've seen the boxes and envelopes in the back. You get packages and mail here all the time from them."

"You're right. It's a company out of Chicago that I have an interest in."

"So you are the one funding the lake project?"

"Partially, there's really a conglomeration of companies involved. So what?"

"And you're the one who bought up all of Old Man Tranchant's land?"

He laughed halfheartedly and went over to his jacket on the coat hanger in the corner. He fumbled through the pockets and pulled out a piece of paper that had been folded many times over. "Let me show you something."

He unfolded a map onto the desk and pointed. "I own everything from the old bridge to the dam on the east side of the creek, except for the five acres that Tranchant's house sits on. It's in some kind of secret trust fund that I haven't been able to touch yet." His long, crabby fingers glided over the map, circling the area in red that he'd colored in. "Just think, Newbie, this will all be yours and Angie's someday."

I didn't say a word. I couldn't. So many questions were running through my brain: Should I take the golden ticket on the table and live a life of luxury? Could I go to the authorities and try to link him to Lonny's murder? Or should I just get the hell out of there before I said the wrong thing?

My silence made him jittery so he folded up the map, placed it inside his jacket pocket, tossed it over a chair, and asked, "Newbie, I need to know where you stand. Are you in or not?"

There it was; he was calling me out. It was time to either go all-in or fold up my hand. Anyone in his right mind would have just said yes and let it be. After all, Alistair, on a whole, had treated me pretty well. I just couldn't imagine what Dante had said about him could be true. But maybe, I just didn't want it to be true.

I don't know what got into me next. Something inside just didn't feel right, and I needed answers. I couldn't see how I'd be able to go on working there without clearing up a few things. Otherwise, I'd be running away from my problems for the rest of my life. No, it was time to make a stand.

"I need to ask you one more question: Lonny Nack, his death wasn't an accident, was it?"

He chuckled and said, "My God, son, what makes you think that?"

"The night Lonny died…" My throat tightened as I swallowed the last ounce of courage I had left.

"Go on," he blurted.

"When Lonny died, you were there, weren't you?"

"Of course I was. You saw me."

"No, I mean, you were there earlier. Before the ambulance arrived."

He slowly reached into another pocket and said, "What makes you think that?"

"Because someone saw you."

"The only people who saw me were the ambulance drivers."

"No, someone else saw you, before they arrived. You pushed the truck in the water, didn't you?"

Alistair Dukas planted both feet and stood as firm as a Redwood tree bracing for a windstorm. With an air of defiance, he replied, "That's a lie."

I paused for a moment to let his words sink in. Not for me, but for him. I could tell by the way the sentence tapered off that he knew that I knew he was lying. He slowly glared down at me with a set of bushy eyebrows that sprouted out of his forehead like a barbwire fence. The scent of roasted coffee lingered around his mouth as he formed his next words. "If what you say is true, then why am I not in jail?"

I wasn't sure what to say next. He had a valid point. He could tell I was grasping for straws, as he'd shot a huge hole into my theory. The only thing I could do was try to put the fear of being caught back in his mind. "Maybe you will be soon."

Without warning, he turned as if to walk away and then swung his hand as hard as he could. The blow caught my chin and sent me tumbling over a chair. Then he reached down and grabbed me by the shirt. A large carving knife came out of his pocket, and he held it to my throat. "That was the wrong thing to say, you stupid boy. You could've had it all."

I inconspicuously slipped the scissors out of my back pocket and plunged them into his arm. While he screamed in agony, I spun away from the knife and tried to get to my feet. As I stood up and turned to run, a jolt of sharp pain shot out of my shoulder blade. It hurt even more when he pulled the knife out as the jagged teeth on the backside of the blade rippled through my skin. I kept hobbling away as he lunged forward again. This time, my arm stopped the blow just enough to keep it from penetrating my body, but I fell hard to the ground.

Alistair stood over me like a vulture sizing up which limb it was going to tear apart first. His scornful eyes flung daggers at me as I tried to recover. I was in a corner of the store, away from the windows with no escape.

"Well, what am I going to do with you?" He twisted the knife in the air. "I could carve you up like a fish and dispose of your body at the dam, but that would take all night. I could pour gasoline on you and just set this whole place on fire...but that's already been done. Two similar deaths in one town might raise suspicions."

"Old Man Tranchant. You killed him too?"

"What was I supposed to do? The old fart wouldn't sell me his land. The tree-hugging environmentalist. He didn't want anything to happen to his precious little valley. A lot of good it's doing him now. Sometimes you have to take matters into your own hands for the greater good. He just couldn't see the big picture."

I wanted to reply that maybe he saw an even bigger picture about what a lake would do to the land but decided not to provoke him any more than I had already. "But why Lonny? What did he do to you?"

He grinned. "The little shit has been a thorn in my side ever since he started working in his father's store. I almost went bankrupt because of that kid. Then there was his constant dumpster diving. I caught him looking at some papers one night and scared him away. I'm pretty sure he knew what I was up to, so I took advantage of the opportunity before he had a chance to do anything about it. That's how you get ahead in this world, son. Do you need more reasons?"

"No, that'll be enough," came a voice from the back of the store. Standing in the shadows next to the boxes was Hightower.

"Why Tony, how...what are you doing here?"

Hightower slowly walked up with a revolver in his hand. "I started to put two and two together this morning after reading the newspaper. I remembered what Colonel Entwhistle said when he gave a statement about the fire...how he told us that he saw you there and sent you to get help. I couldn't understand, for the life of me, what you were doing there in the first place. Then I went by the dam today to look over the accident site and ran into Mr. McIntosh. He had a stringer of fish and asked if I wanted to buy any. That got me thinking about the accident. Why didn't his son have any fish when we found him? The only answer I could come up with was that maybe he'd already sold them to his favorite customer. And that would be you, Alistair...meaning that you were there before the accident occurred. You could have pushed Lonny's truck into the water and slipped away before anyone knew it."

Mr. Dukas dropped the knife to the ground "You got me, Tony. You can either arrest me or go into business with me. All we have to do is get rid of this punk here, and we're good to go. My family is out of town for a few days, so I have all night to figure this out. We could ship him up to Chicago, you know, 'Special Delivery Style.' The boys up there have a way of making things disappear, if you know what I mean." He smirked. "Nobody would ever know."

"I suppose you'll sell me back my house, too, at no cost. I bet you also planned that one out, didn't you. You were probably the one all along who nudged the State's Attorney to get rid of me, now that I think about it. I know it wasn't Ferny or the mayor." Hightower cocked the trigger. "I may be a lot of things, Alistair, but a murderer and cheat I'm not. I don't care how much I despise this kid and his little band of misfits. So, put your hands up in the air, and shut up before I shoot you myself."

"Okay, okay. For Pete's sake, let me grab my coat first."

Alistair strolled over to the coat rack and lifted off a jacket. Hightower knelt down to look at my wound. "You gonna be alright, kid?"

"Yeah, I think so."

"Let me call for an ambulance." As he picked up the receiver and began dialing, he motioned to Dukas. "Get over here where I can see you better."

"I'm coming."

Alistair slowly placed both arms in the sleeves and adjusted his collar. Hightower kept one eye on him while fumbling around with the dial on the telephone. It was right then that I noticed Mr. Dukas's other coat sitting on the chair. Then, in that split second before I could get a word out, when Hightower glanced down to find the right number, a knife came out from behind Dukas's head. It silently cut a path through the air, twirling like a baton until it landed in Hightower's chest. The chief dropped the receiver and clutched the blade as blood began to trickle out. A moment later, the gun fell to his side. With each heartbeat, another finger slipped off the handle until it tumbled onto the floor. Soon Hightower was on his knees, praying for another breath, angling for elevation, until his shoulders finally hit the ground.

Alistair Dukas's grin widened as he picked the carving knife off the floor, walked over, and pulled the other blade out of Hightower's chest. He wiped it clean with his handkerchief and said, "Did I ever tell you about the summer I spent traveling with the circus? Oh Newbie, you would've loved it. I mean, it was only three months, and we just stayed in the tri-state area, but still, it was an adventure. As luck would have it, one of the regulars there took a liking to me and taught me a few things about throwing knives. It's quite an art, contrary to what most people believe. Not just anyone can learn it. You have to have, how should I say it: talent."

He spun around on his heels, with the handle secured in his right hand and his pointer finger lying on top of the blade. "Take for instance, throwing a knife with no spin. All it takes is bending your elbow at 90 degrees and a flick of the wrist." With that, the blade darted across the room like an arrow, landing two inches away from my head. When I reached up to grab it, another knife came out of his pocket and sailed toward me with blinding speed. It landed between the first knife and my nose.

"Now, now, now, Newbie. Don't spoil the show."

He leisurely walked over and pulled the knives out of the wall. I felt weak from the blood loss and struggled to keep my eyes open. In my back pocket was the box cutter, but what good was that going to do against twelve-inch blades?

Alistair paced the floor. "I can take the van out back. Both of you will fit in there nicely. It's a good four-hour drive to Chicago so I should make some coffee for the trip." He removed the lid off the percolator and took it over to the sink. "How do you like your coffee, Newbie, cream, sugar, stirred with a twist of steel?"

As he turned on the faucet and filled up the percolator, I slowly slid across the floor toward the telephone. The receiver was dangling over the edge of the desk just a few feet away. The sound of the water drowned out any noise my shoes made on the wooden floor. When I was close enough to reach it, I realized that resetting the phone and dialing the operator was not going to be easy without drawing attention. Mr. Dukas began humming as he opened a coffee can and added grinds to the filter. It was now or never.

I slipped a quarter out of my pocket and tossed it to the back of the store. Alistair went completely silent as his head whipped around and followed the sound. He sat down the filter and slowly crept toward the back room. When he turned away from me, I reached up for the phone. Just then, a knife whizzed through the air and landed in my shirtsleeve pinning me to the desk.

"That's more like it. Let's make this interesting. What good's a knife fight without a little drama? I'll tell you what. I'll go and make sure the back door is locked while you try to hide. How's that sound?"

As soon as he left the room, I tore my sleeve away from the knife and pushed down the button on the telephone. Just before I could dial zero, another knife struck the side of the phone and sent it tumbling over the front of the desk.

"I thought for sure you would've gone for the knife first. And to think, I was going to let you marry my daughter. Boy, was that ever a mistake." He checked his watch. "Well, this game is growing old fast. I think I'll need to make this quick and easy."

He walked over to where I was leaning against the desk and grabbed me by the hair. "No, cutting the throat would make too much of a mess out here. I think we need to move this into the bathroom."

And with that, he dragged me across the floor while I kicked and screamed, "Help, anyone. Help!" I dug into my back pocket for the box cutter, pulled it out, and slashed it across his wrist.

"Damn you, boy!" Mr. Dukas released me, stepped back, and placed his handkerchief over the wound. "You're not making this any easier. I guess we'll just have to do it right here."

He twirled the carving knife in his right hand and swung it back, ready to strike when a bullet blasted into the back of his head. The sound echoed off the front windows, rattling them just enough to be heard. His head bobbed sideways as his limp body spilled forward and hit the ground hard. I immediately grabbed the knife off the floor and waited for any movement. Nothing came.

Over a few feet to the right was Hightower leaning on his elbow with the revolver in hand. His other hand was covering the wound in his chest. He watched Dukas fall and then peered over to me. For a moment, his grip tightened around the handle and the gun swayed in the air crossing from one end of the desk to the other where I lie. I could almost feel the internal squabble being debated inside his head as his eyes stared right through me, judging whether I was worth keeping alive or not. The tip of the pistol dipped, and he asked, "Do you think you can use the phone?" I nodded as his eyes closed and head dropped onto his arm.

I was at the hospital for days. Vague memories of nurses checking my blood pressure and poking tubes in my arm were all that I could recall. The county sheriff came in on the second day after they weaned me off the sedatives and asked for a statement. With my father by my side, I tried to recall every detail. The whole county was buzzing with rumors about what had happened since everyone involved was either dead or out cold. I'm sure there was a reporter waiting outside my door, trying to get any kind of information from the sheriff when he left. Hightower survived the ordeal but spent the next two weeks between the Emergency Room, O.R., and Intensive Care. He'd barely escaped death as the knife wound had only punctured one of his lungs. Alistair Dukas was D.O.A.

They wouldn't let anyone visit me while in the hospital, so I was glad to be released and placed into my father's care. The boys were waiting on the front porch as I carefully scooted out of the car and made my way up the drive. Sally was there too. I don't remember much of what we talked about, as things were still a bit hazy from the medications. I kept nodding off so they put me to bed and left early.

That next morning, I woke up in a cold sweat just before dawn. I kept seeing Lonny's body being lifted out of the water by the paramedics. His head tilted back, beckoning the stars and celestial bodies to welcome him in. Even in death, he had more charisma than most of the living. "No blood, no foul," he was saying. Hopefully, with my blood, his soul would finally get the vindication it needed to move on.

After the third call from the news media, my dad just took the phone off the hook. He knew that I needed time to heal. The next morning, he smiled and placed the newspaper on the kitchen table without saying a word. After reading the article about Hightower and Alistair, I noticed another story at the top of the local section of the paper. The headline read, "Local Discount Store Overrun By Feral Cats." The article said that more than ten wild cats had gotten into Dukas's Emporium overnight and destroyed several pieces of merchandise. I just shook my head as I envisioned Charlie Springer herding a group of cats from the lake to the back of Dukas's store. I guess he finally felt vindicated, too.

All I did for the next few days was sleep and watch television. Officer Hightower was being portrayed as a hero. The one who'd exposed a dastardly scheme of murder while saving another victim from imminent death. It had all the makings of high TV drama with murder, corruption, and heroics. Watching it night after night felt like an out-of-body experience. Hearing my name in the reports and listening to the newscasters try to describe my role in the story, inferring this and that, was almost comical.

Hightower was reinstated as Chief of Police in Bunsen Creek a few weeks later. Angie and her family had already slipped out of town and disappeared. Soon afterward, I got a postcard from New York that just read, "I'm sorry." All of Alistair's property was seized by the state until the courts could decide what to do with it. The paper speculated that most of the land would be deeded over to the county so the lake project could continue. Even Hightower was given a chance to buy back his old house.

I got a call from Sally around the end of the month. It was her eighteenth birthday, and she wanted me to come over and eat some cake. We'd talked on the phone a little bit about Lonny's murder since I'd come home, but for some reason, she didn't want to know all the details. I guess she had moved on. She said that she missed talking with me. Not only did I agree, I felt a gaping hole inside open back up. With her words, every emotion that I'd locked away during the past year or so had resurfaced.

I fired up my trusty motorcycle and took off racing down the street. When I came up to the stop sign, my hand unconsciously squeezed the brake handle bringing me to a complete stop. I'm not sure why either. I could've probably run every sign through town and gotten away with it, but I didn't want to. Something had changed. Even though I knew Hightower would never chase me again, I had no desire to tempt him. We had bonded. We were united by circumstances for the rest of our lives, and silly little things like running stop signs seemed so meaningless from then on.

When I arrived, Sally was at the table with her father and Mrs. Blanche. Throughout everything, they'd evolved into a bona fide family unit. It may have been a bit atypical, but it worked all the same. Mrs. Blanche lit the candles on the cake, and we sang. Ice cream was served on top, and everyone had coffee to wash it down.

Sally and I sat on the porch and caught up on all the news. I did most of the talking as she held my hand and listened. When we were done with the gory details and local gossip, she pulled out a document, opened it up, and said, "You won't believe the birthday present I got today."

As I unfolded the papers and started reading, she added, "It's a deed to Old Man Tranchant's place, and you'll never guess where it came from."

"From Lonny."

"How'd you know?"

Visions of Buzzard's tale about a wrapped-up pulsating bomb being placed into a bank teller's window came to mind. Only after Lonny had gotten the money and was far enough away from the scene of the crime did the police arrive. Then it was discovered that inside the bag he'd left was a buzzing vibrator. I just shook my head and said, "It's a long story."

Sally just nodded. "Another time then."

I looked up. "What are you going to do with the place?"

"Oh, I don't know. Something tells me that Lonny didn't buy it just so it could become a lake." She gazed into my eyes and sighed. "It really bothers me not knowing what he'd want me to do with the place. There was no note or nothing."

I rubbed her hand and said, "You know, what bothers me the most about Lonny?"

"No, what?"

"I never did have a chance to play harmonica with him."

"Really?"

"I mean, it was one of those things we kept saying we'd do but, you know, never got around to doing. I feel a bit guilty because I kind of avoided playing with him for the longest time. I guess I was a bit embarrassed about how bad I was…and how good he was. I just kept putting it off, thinking that the perfect time to get together would eventually come on its own."

She looked out into the yard and sighed. "Yes, life is full of lost opportunities and second chances."

"Do you remember what Lonny said that day right here on this porch? You know, right before he streaked through town. I do, and I'll never forget it. He said, 'There are those who walk on two feet, and others like me that run on all four.'" I grabbed both her hands and stared into her eyes. "I don't want to be like the others, Sally. I want to run on all four."

"And do what, Newbie?"

"I don't know yet. Maybe steal a cop car or streak through the middle of town."

Sally brushed back my bangs. "You don't have to be like Lonny. That was his thing. There was a reason why he was like that."

"What do you mean?"

"I mean, Lonny had a rare disease called Huntington's Chorea. He didn't think I knew about it, but I saw an article circled in a magazine in his room one day. Then I went to the library and looked it up." She blinked back a tear and continued, "He had all of the symptoms: slurred speech, problems swallowing, spastic eye movements, impulsiveness, you name it. It was just a matter of time."

"Wow, I didn't think you knew."

"What do you mean, I didn't know?"

I squeezed her hand. "A couple of years ago, right after he got out of jail, Lonny ran into me at the diner. He told me about how your mother died and that she had the same disease. Then he said there was a 50/50 chance that you'd get it too."

"Why would he tell you that and not me?"

"I guess he didn't want you to worry…and he saw the way I looked at you. He knew I was in love and didn't want me to break your heart later on when, I mean if the symptoms started showing up."

Sally was speechless. I could tell that she was struggling with all of this new information, trying to piece together conversations and the lack of them in the past. "That sounds about right. Lonny was weird that way. He thought he could protect me from all of the world's problems and keep me safe." This thought brought a slight grin to her face as she added, "I knew though. After visiting the library that day, I knew that Mama had the same disease. Nobody would come out and tell me, but I could see it in their faces."

I could also see in her face that the layers of uncertainty were finally being peeled away. I couldn't imagine living with such a predicament. All of my troubles and worries seemed so pale in comparison now. Yet, I couldn't have wanted to be with her more.

"Sally, I don't want this to be another lost opportunity. I mean, with us. Do you think we can have a second chance?"

She kissed me on the cheek. "You silly fool. You were always the one."

"And you too. You know, I can still get a job in the coal mines, and maybe we can move in together…out at Old Man Tranchant's place."

She put her hand over my mouth and then kissed me. I inhaled the scent of her skin and ran my fingers gently through her hair. Being with her had never felt so right. In that brief moment, I knew what I wanted to do for the rest of my life.

"You'll do nothing of the sort," she said. "You are going to the U of I, and you are going to graduate with high honors. Then, if you feel the same way on down the road, we'll talk about the future. Besides, I have plans of my own, you know."

"Plans, what kind of plans?"

"Well, I've been thinking about everything that's happened, with Lonny and the store and all. And I finally realized that I needed a change in my life."

I nodded as she continued, "So I went down to city hall and had a nice long heart to heart talk with Chief Hightower. I mean, there had been a lot of bad blood between him and Lonny, and I just wanted it to all go away."

"You've got to be kidding. What'd he say?"

"He knew about what Billy had done to me. I guess his little brother confessed after the accident, believing that it was an omen or sign from God, and he just wanted to come clean." Her eyes watered up as she sniffled. "I'm sorry. It's just still hard to talk about it."

I rubbed her hand. "I can't imagine."

She wiped away the tears with her sleeve. "Anyway, the next thing you know, he offered to help me prepare for the exam."

"What exam?"

"The exam that I have to pass in order to go to the Police Academy. I want to become a State Trooper or maybe a Secret Service Agent. You never know. Heck, I may even become a lawyer."

"Holy moly! What brought this on?"

"I don't know. I think it's been there inside of me all along, but I just didn't realize it until now. You know, the way I was in school with Billy Hightower and not letting him push us around."

"You didn't let anybody push you around."

"Watch yourself. I may be pulling you over someday."

"Point taken."

She glided her hair behind her ear and sighed. "And then there's Lonny. I loved him to death, but something tells me that if the right person had been there for him at the right time, maybe he wouldn't have been as crazy as he was..."

I cut her off. "...Or maybe he was just born that way."

She smiled. "Point taken. Yeah, I'm sure the disease had plenty to do with the way he acted and all. You know, living every day like it was his last." Then she straightened up. "Anyway, I just know that this is the first thing I've really wanted to do for years, and, as Lonny would say, 'Carpe diem.'"

"Carpe diem. I have to remember that one."

I couldn't have loved her more in that moment, and I told her so. Those three words that I hadn't uttered since Mother was alive.

I guess this was the first time since then that I'd really felt that way about another person…and it felt good.

On the ride back home, I kept thinking about Lonny. He'd been running on four legs, metaphorically, his whole life. Answering the call of the wild within and never letting anything hold him back. But for me, it was different. I didn't have that kind of yearning desire. Yet, I didn't want to be like the others.

Yes, it was all there in front of me now. That connecting point, you could say, where my next journey was beginning and where it would eventually lead me, leaping into another world of uncertainty. That place where reality ends and imagination begins. No, there weren't any others like me. There never had been, and there never would be. That was the greater meaning of Lonny's words. The sooner I realized that and went about being myself, the sooner everything else would turn out for the best. And somewhere in between that absurd random set of occurrences we call life, I finally realized that in order to feel alive, I had to quit seeking out its meaning and just *live*.

Thank you, Lonny.

As the weeks went by, Sally and I had the chance to reconnect. We spent the rest of the summer talking about the future and laughing about the past. This made leaving for college even more difficult than anticipated. In reality though, the university wasn't that far away so anytime either one of us needed to refuel, we could be in each other's arms within an hour or so. The day finally came when I had to throw some clothes and cash in a backpack, grab my toothbrush, and head off for college. I'd never felt so right about something in my life. Yes, I was now running on all four.

All four cylinders, that is.

About The Author

Thomas Lopinski grew up in a quaint small town in Illinois called Georgetown with one stoplight, one high school, one square, one lake, one police car, and one hundred ways to get into trouble. It was a wonderful place to be a child. He studied at the University of Illinois and later moved to Southern California with his wife and children to work in the music business. He is also a member of the Independent Writers of Southern California (IWOSC). His first novel, *Document 512*, won several awards and recognition in 2012-2013 from Readers View Reviewers Choice Awards, Best Indie Book Awards, IndieFab Awards and the National Indie Excellence Book Awards.

Made in the USA
Charleston, SC
29 September 2015